Stephanie P.

A HUSTLER'S WORST NIGHTMARE

A NOVEL BY

DERRICK KING

D0904368

Editor: Todd Hunter
                            Literary Consultant Group
Photographer: Howard Huang
Cover Concept &
  Publishing Consultant: Nakea S. Murray
                            Literary Consultant Group
Cover Design: Dashawn Taylor
                            www.ultimatemediahosting.com
Book Layout: Shawna A. Grundy
                            sag@shawnagrundy.com

ISBN10: 0-981-784-003
ISBN13: 978-098-1784-007

ACKNOWLEDGEMENTS

First of all, I have to give praise to my higher power, and thank Him for allowing me to find my gift in life. Trust me, we all have a gift we just can't give up finding it.

To my beautiful mom, Karen King, your baby boy finally did it. I love you so much. I hope you're proud of me.

To my daughter Shayna King(Mutta), you're my inspiration in life. I couldn't ask for a better child. Keep doing what you're doing because the sky is the limit.

To Carol Tucker, thank you for always believing in me. You'll always hold a place in my heart, I love you.

To Dame and Dwan, even though we're cousins we grew up as brothers. Thanks for long-filled Hennessy nights.

To the rest of my cousins, Dawud, Saudia, Suliaman, Sabria, Yazmin, Rasheed, Huriyyah, Mahdiah, Taahiah, Khatim, Amir, Liyana, Ihsan , Merrick, Tony, and Nikki I love you all.

To my aunts Zakiah, Gail, Donna, Porchia, and Trecie thanks for everything.

To my uncle Abul-Latif, we grew up as brothers thanks for teaching me how to hustle.

To my grandparents Larry Watkins, Eddie & Margaret Battle I love you all.

To my brother Gary King thanks for all the nieces and nephew I know you're not done yet ☺.

To the Scrivens and Tucker families you are truly the best. To the Boyer Family, I love you all.

Now to the streets, I want start off first by saying rest in peace. To all my homies that became victims to the streets, they're too many to name, but know you're always in my thoughts. To my homies that fell victim to the system, keep ya'll heads up, don't let them lams or nut ass C.O.'s knock you off your square.

To my squad, T, Silk, Black, Big Mont, Den, Suga Ray, John, Cell, Bates, BC Money, Ev, Kirk, and the rest of the squad ya'll know what it is. To the whole Euclid St. squad, and the whole Wynnefield squad, keep holding things down in the hood.

To that hot author Nicolette, who has a couple of the hottest books out there, (Paper Doll and Friction) thanks for believing in me. Before you even knew if I could write or not, you knew one hand washes the other. I definitely owe you one. We're going to take the game by storm.

To Nakea Murray, you are truly a blessing. Thank you for making this book come together as smoothly and stress-free as possible. Yes sir! ☺

I would like to thank the rest of the people that helped me make my dream come true, Todd Hunter, Editor; Shawna Grundy, Typesetter; and Cindy Carter, Typist.

Anybody else I might have forgotten…sorry cuss me out later!

This book is dedicated to my grandmother
Cecelia Watkins

And my father
Gary King

I Love You Both
May you rest in peace...

A WOLF MAY COME IN SHEEP'S CLOTHING

Slick bitches play the role of a shiestey nigga/getting low down and dirty like a trifling nigga/it could even be ya wifey nigga...

Just schemin' wit they eyes on ya riches, when they think you sleepin/the snakes will come out of the trenches...

Them chicks will take over ya mind, body and soul/cause when it comes to money, they always lose control...

And it's a good chance the chick will leave ya man killed/cause the plan was goin strait/then it turned into left field...

Her whole plan was to tie you up or something/and clean ya whole stash out and leave you wit nothin...

It's a Hustla's worst nightmare, so watch them snakes/cause when the time is right, their gonna take ya cake...

"Stay on point, because you could be next..."

PROLOGUE

Pop-pop-pop-pop! Buc-buc-buc-buc!

"Damn…I'm out of bullets," Big Toe yelled checking the clip on his .40 caliber handgun.

"Shit, me too!" said his partner Flea sweating profusely. Big Toe ducked his head lower behind a parked car.

"Man, what we gonna do? I can feel the bullets flying pass my ear!" Flea said as he clutched the bag he held in his hand. "These dudes really tryin to kill us."

"Man we just robbed dem cats for six kilos and a duffel bag full of money. I'd be trying to kill us too!" Big Toe said as he tried to figure out his next move.

"Well look, we need to make a run for it. So which way you runnin?" Flea asked, looking from side to side.

"Shit man, do it really matter?"

"Hell yeah it matters!" Flea said ready to make his move.

"Nigga,why it matter so much, when bullets is flying everywhere?" Big Toe asked as he heard bullets hitting the other side of the car where they were hiding.

"Nigga, it matters because I don't want to run your big slow ass over," Flea explained with a smile on his face.

"Don't worry bout dat, just worry bout getting to the car."

"Aight look, I'll run out first. I need you right behind me cause we gonna make it to this car." Flea said, squating in the sprint position.

"Homie, I'll be right on ya heels, trust me." Big Toe said as he grabbed the straps on the duffel bag that held the money.

Pop-pop-pop-pop-pop!

"The bullets stopped," Flea said.

"That's because they're probably reloading. So get up now and run nigga."

Flea got up with the bag of six kilos and ran to the car like a runaway slave. Big Toe surprised Flea by being only a couple steps behind. With Big Toe's 260 pound frame, no one would expect him to run so fast. They ran past six cars and the bullets started flying again.

"We almost there," Flea said, ducking his head never losing one stride in his step.

"You don't think I know dat?" Big Toe asked, knowing they would be home free if they made it to the car.

"Agghh! I think something bit me on my leg," Flea screamed. He grabbed the back of his leg and his stride slowed.

"You shot, but don't slow up now." Big Toe demanded as he placed his arm around Flea's back helping him to the car.

"Man it feels like my leg is on fire," Flea said, limping the rest of the way to the car.

"You're goin to be aight. Wit all this money we got you can buy yourself a new leg."

They threw the bag with the six kilos of coke and the duffel bag of money through an open back window of the car.

"Can you drive?" Big Toe asked Flea while helping him into the car.

"Shit, do I like porkchops and white women?" Flea asked, sliding over to the driver's side.

"Yeah you can drive. But I told you before, if these bullets don't kill you, dem porkchops and white women will. Now push dat gas pedal to the floor!"

Flea turned the key that was already in the ignition and the car came to life. He put the car into drive, turned the wheel, and made a left out of the parking spot.

Out of nowhere a gun was held inside the car. The gunman squeezed the trigger of his .38 caliber revolver.

Pop-pop-pop-pop!

Big Toe was hit three times in the chest, and Flea was hit once in the knee cap. Flea kept driving as bullets continued to hit the car.

"Yo Toe, you aight?" Flea asked while turning left at the corner followed by a right at the following corner. "Toe! Talk to me family." Flea screamed, reaching over shaking Big Toe.

"I'm dyin," Big Toe managed to mumble.

"Fuck that. You ain't dyin on me. I'm a get you to the hospital."

"Flea...listen to me. I never felt death before, but I know I'm feeling it now. I...I need you to do me a favor."

"You know I will do anything for you. You ain't goin die though...you can't die." Flea said, trying to make it to the nearest hospital.

"Listen...I...I need you to...to take care of my girls for me. You...you know I'm all they got...since their mother died. I don't want my babies growing up separately in foster homes."

Big Toe's eyes were opening and closing as he fought for life.

"You know I love dem girls, like they was my own. You never have to worry bout dat."

Flea turned left knowing he was only five minutes away from the hospital.

"We...we was always like brothers, huh? I love you Flea."

Flea pulled into the hospital parking lot.

"Come on Toe, these doctors gonna fix you up."

Flea looked over at Big Toe and saw his eyes open. Even though his eyes were open, he knew Big Toe was already gone.

"I love you too Big Toe," Flea said sadly with a tear rolling down his face.

Flea reached over and closed Big Toe's eyes for good...

CHAPTER 1

Twenty years later. It's 1999.

"Uhhmm yeah, right there boy." Stori instructed Keith as he performed oral sex on her.

They both sat in Stori's brand new Cadillac Escalade. She sat in the driver's seat with her back against the door and her right leg thrown across the top of the passenger's headrest. Her left foot was propped up on the dashboard as she let Keith handle his business.

"Uhhmm, you like how dat shit taste, don't you?" She said grabbing the back of Keith's head pulling his face further into her vagina.

"Umm...hmm, you taste like a watermelon Laffy Taffy." He muttered, barely able to get the words out with a mouth full of Stori's juices.

"Damn boy...if you don't know how to do shit else right in your life, you sure know how to eat dis pussy right." Stori said biting her bottom lip ready to climax. Keith threw his tongue into overdrive as Stori's leg started to shake. "Yeah boy...drink all this shit." Stori demanded as she climaxed in Keith's mouth.

Keith licked up every last drop of Stori's juices as she held her head back against the window with her eyes closed.

Stori opened her eyes and lifted her head to see Keith with his pants down by his ankles and his manhood standing at attention.

"Boy, what da fuck are you doin? Did I tell you to pull your dick out?" Stori said angrily while reaching in her back seat.

She pulled out some baby wipes and started cleaning up her private parts.

"But I thought…"

"But you thought…what? See…there you go thinking again. What…you thought you was getting some pussy? Cause I know you aint think I was suckin your dick." Stori said, as she slid her Victoria Secret thong over her voluptuous ass and straightened out her Coogi dress.

"I'm saying you let me taste you, so I figured you'll let me feel you too." Keith explained pulling his pants up as his penis started to go limp.

"I swear y'all niggas kill me thinking yall God's gift to women. I'm here to tell you, I'm man's worst fuckin nightmare."

Keith held a confused look on his face with his left eyebrow raised.

Ring…ring…ring!

"Hello, oh what's up sis?"

"I need you to come through, so I can show you our next victim. I swear dis nigga in here got more ice on than Baby from Cash Money."

"Diamond hold on. Look Kevin."

"My name is Keith." "Kevin, Keith…same thing. I got to take care of some business right now, so you gotta go."

"You ain't gonna take me home," Keith said, looking pitiful.

"Naw…take this $20 and catch a cab or something." Stori pulled a $20 bill out of her Chanel clutch bag.

"FUCK YOU BITCH! I don't have to take this shit." Keith opened the passenger door to step down from the truck.

"I'm the baddest bitch you gonna ever come across," Stori explained as she winked at Keith.

Keith slammed the door, and Stori pulled off in her Escalade leaving Keith standing on the sidewalk.

"Hello Diamond…yeah I'm back."

"Stori, who was that you was talking greasy to?" Diamond asked, knowing that's how her sister was.

"That nigga Keith from up West Oak Lane," Stori answered. She reached into her ashtray to grab her neatly rolled blunt and lit it up.

"You talkin about Keith with the hazel eyes and curly hair. Girl he fine as shit. Why you do em like that?"

"Girl you know how I get down. These niggas been treating females dirty for years. I ain't doin nothing but flippin the script. You know I don't love dem ho's."

Diamond laughed hard on the other line at her sister's comment.

"Girl you crazy, just get your ass up here quick. I got Alize' in there holding him down, but I don't know how long he's gonna stay."

"I'll be there in twenty minutes. Bye bitch." Stori playfully said to her sister.

She turned on Jay-Z's *Hard Knock Life* song and drove up Broad Street to Night On Broadway, an after hours go-go club that stayed open until 5 a.m. Fifteen minutes later Stori walked down the steps of the dim smoke filled club. The place was packed with all the ballers and tricks of Philadelphia. The baller's from Uptown had a strong presence, because Night on Broadway is in their part of town. Stori spotted her sister Diamond and made her way through the crowd.

"What's up girl?" Stori asked walking up on Diamond.

"Waitin on you," Diamond said, standing in the corner next to the stage where the dancers performed.

"It's hotter than a mu'fucka up in here. What they got the heat on, Africa?" Stori asked fanning her face with her hand.

"Girl, it ain't that hot in here, but here…you can have my spring water."

Stori opened the water and lifted the bottle to her lips. She drank nearly all of the water leaving only a little in the bottle. She

7

handed the bottle back to Diamond.

"What da hell am I suppose to do wit dis?"

"My bad. That purple haze got my mouth dry as shit." Stori confessed as she applied lip gloss to her full lips.

"You better have some of that purple left for me...Stori I know you hear me."

"Yeah...yeah girl, I hear you, but I know this girl ain't ready to stick that full bottle of Heineken up her pussy?" Stori replied, while watching the girl on stage open up a fresh Heineken bottle, squat over it, and insert it into her vagina.

The ballers in the club went wild flooding the stage with one dollar bills. The stripper then laid on her back with the Heineken bottle halfway inside her. Every body watched the beer drain out from inside the stripper's vagina. The crowd became even more wild and rowdy.

Stori stood to the side with her mouth open not believing what she was witnessing. After the beer bottle was completely emptied, the stripper finally pulled it out of her vagina. She then stood up and made her butt cheeks clap. Everybody in the crowd had a confused look on their face wondering where all the beer went. The stripper turned her back to the crowd, bent over, and beer came spraying out of her vagina. The ballers emptied their pockets and money seemed to rain from the ceiling.

"That's a good muthafuckin Heineken she wastin," said one of the guys in the crowd. He jumped on stage, opened his mouth and tried to drink the beer coming out of the stripper's vagina. After the stripper did her beer trick, Stori was speechless and suddenly thought she was going to be sick. She grabbed Diamond's arm and pulled her away from the stage. Diamond prepared herself for a big lecture, but she was surprised when it didn't come. Diamond read her eyes and knew exactly what Stori was thinking. She just didn't want to hear any shit from Stori.

"I don't care, I'm grown," Diamond thought, as she challenged

Stori's stare.

Diamond was the baby of five sisters. They were all beautiful women, but Diamond's deep-set dimples made her stand out. At the age of twenty-one she was every man and boy's dream. She had her mother's flawless golden brown complexion. Standing at 5'6" and thick in all the right places, Diamond was known to hold up traffic. Guys couldn't get over how small her waist was considering she had an ass like Serena Williams. Needless to say, she was a dime.

"So where dis nigga at so we can get out of here. You know I can't stand it up in here," Stori said, wishing her baby sister would find something else to do. "I still don't understand how you be in here."

"Girl, stop hatin' on my profession and that nigga I was talking about is over there," Diamond said, pointing at a guy across the room that was covered in sparkling diamonds.

Stori stared at the guy with all the ice as he got a lap dance. "Yeah, I think we might be on to something," she confessed.

"Girl you know I know money when I see it and I know this nigga gotta be large," Diamond said, getting Stori's blood pumping even more. "All the money he's been kicking out tonight will probably be enough to pay every stripper in here house rent at the end of the month."

"It's on." Stori said.

Stori felt hypnotized from the sparkling diamonds that covered their next victim's fingers, wrist, and neck.

"Damn Temptation…who dis wit you?" A drunk guy mumbled who knew Diamond only by her stage name.

"Oh…you really don't want to know that." Diamond said to the drunk while Stori just stood there with her nose turned up.

"I'm sayin Temptation, she's just as fine as your ass and since I can't have none of you, what's up wit her?" The drunk asked, pulling out $1,000 dollars.

Stori with her bowlegged legs and her Coogi dress stood

there like a star. The drunk was right. Stori was just as beautiful as Diamond. Actually if the guy wasn't so drunk, he would have seen that Stori and Diamond looked just alike. The only difference is that Stori is two inches shorter than Diamond. She has her father's dark skin complexion that makes her look like a sweet Hershey's candy bar.

Stori wanted to scream and embarrass the drunk but she didn't want to bring unwanted attention to herself. She was strictly there for business.

"Look, why don't you put your little money away. It ain't that type of party," Stori said as calm as she could.

"It ain't that type of party, huh? This is some bullshit. All ya'll dick teasers up in here," the drunk said, stuffing money in his back pocket and walking off.

"See this is the trifling shit I'm talking bout. That's exactly why I be shittin on these lame ass niggas out here. And I don't know why guys think...if they pull out a couple dollars, we suppose to bow down or something," Stori complained over the loud music. "Like females can't make their own money. That's why this degrading shit in here be making me sick to my stomach."

Diamond didn't respond. She just stood there shaking her head up and down as Stori vented.

"Look, let's sit out front and wait on the guy with all the ice... before I fuck around and have to shoot somebody in here."

"Aight, let me go in the back, so I can grab my bag."

Five minutes later Stori and Diamond were walking toward the front door of the club. The club was still packed, so they had to squeeze pass people to get by.

"Ooh, scuse me," Stori said, bumping hard into the drunk that was talking shit to them earlier. She knocked the drunk's Hennessy all over him.

"BITCH watch where you goin!" The drunk slurred wiping the Hennessy off of his polo shirt.

Stori just blew him a kiss and walked by smiling to herself. Once outside, Stori and Diamond waited across the street from the club in Stori's Escalade. Diamond lit the half smoked blunt that was in the ashtray. She kicked off her Fendi slides and curled her feet up under her.

"Where your Benz at?" Stori asked referring to Diamond's CLK55 Mercedes Benz.

"It's at home. I got Koran to drive me here. He's suppose to pick me up. I'm a call him and tell him never mind though," Diamond explained going through her bag to look for her cell phone.

"You still mess wit dat boy Koran?"

"If you wanna call it that. I still ain't give em none. But he's definitely sticking around. He's so sweet and such a gentleman. He kind of fell into the friend zone." Diamond said, smacking the side of her hip.

"You know I need a thug to pull my hair and smack my ass."

"I hear you on that, but Diamond...why are you still dancing? You got everything you want, plus more, and none of it is from dancing. You need to give dat shit up." Stori said sliding her sunroof back.

"Stori, don't start trippin' on me. You don't have a problem with me dancing when I'm setting up a job for us. Matter fact the majority of our jobs come from me being in go-go bars, so don't be no hypocrite."

"Relax girl, I just be worried about my baby sister. I can't help it if I love and care about you."

"I love you too, but there's no need to worry. You know I stay strapped," Diamond said pulling out her chrome .380 caliber hand gun.

Even though Diamond wasn't trying to hear what Stori was saying, she knew she was right. She didn't know how to tell her sister that she was addicted to dancing. Diamond knew she had everything she ever dreamed of having...a new home, new car, clothes, jewelry, an endless shoe collection, and enough money saved to retire. She didn't dance for the money. She did it for the excitement and she loved the attention even more. Diamond knew her sisters would never understand.

"Besides girl, you don't make no real money in there," Stori continued as she took the blunt from Diamond's hand.

"Well this money right here gonna buy me them Luichiny stilettos I seen for $650. Plus I'm a get this Salvatore Ferragamo purse for $890. Now that sounds like real money to me." Diamond licked her thumb flipping the $1,500 that she made dancing that night.

"It took you, what…a few hours to make that money? That's too time consuming to only make that little bit of money. Now I made this in under five seconds." Stori bragged, pulling out a wad of money.

"Where you make that at?" Diamond asked curiously.

"I made this at your job right before we came out here," Stori said, counting the money in her hand. "I bumped into the back of that drunk ass nigga that was talking shit, dipped in his pocket, and I didn't have to shake my ass once."

"Stori, you pickpocketed that boy? I don't believe you did that."

"What can I say? Uncle Flea taught us well. Besides, I like makin that easy money. I'm not breakin a sweat for nobody to give me a dollar." Stori said, stuffing the money inside her Chanel bag.

Diamond ignored Stori's slick remark. She knew none of her sisters would ever understand that dancing made her feel alive.

"Look Diamond…I think that's him coming out now," Stori said, watching the guy with all the ice jump in his Maserati Quattroporte.

"Damn, that nigga got a Maserati? We might hit the mother load with this one." Diamond said with dollar signs in her eyes.

"You might be right baby sis." Stori started her Escalade.

"That nigga got that Maserati so make sure you keep up wit 'em."

"Don't disrespect my driving skills like that," Stori said, pulling the Escalade behind the Maserati.

A half hour later they were in Moorestown, New Jersey. They watched the Maserati pull up in a long drive way that headed to a mini-mansion.

"What I tell you? Dis nigga paid out da ass." Diamond said excitedly, as she looked at the surroundings.

"We might gotta pull Tori and Zikeema in on this job. No tellin' how much shit he got up in there." Stori said.

"That's a bet...how we gonna do this one?" Diamond asked.

"Let me follow this nigga for a couple weeks. I'm sure I'll come up with something." Stori assured Diamond.

Like Diamond was addicted to dancing, Stori was addicted to robbing people. Just like Diamond, Stori had everything she ever wanted. She owned a condo. She drove a brand new truck and car. She wore all the designer clothes and shoes a woman could ever want. Stori owned eight hair salons, kept a 6 foot safe full of money, and only robbed people because it was in her blood. She felt so alive when she was stickin' somebody up. All of the "ol' heads" told Stori that she reminded them of her father. That would always bring a smile to her face, because her father, Big Toe, was notorious in the stick-up game. Stori wanted to keep his legend alive.

"Damn, it's 5:30 a.m. already? Let's go get some breakfast. Then you can take my ass home." Diamond said, turning on the T.V. inside Stori's dashboard and putting in her favorite movie, *Belly*.

Stori pulled off with one thing on her mind...taking every dime from the guy with all the ice.

CHAPTER 2

Zikeema sat preparing for her mid-terms in her class at Temple University, but she was unable to concentrate. She still couldn't believe that the night before the Philadelphia 76er's lost to the L.A. Clippers.

"I don't know why I even bet on them bum ass Sixers," Zikeema thought. Now she owed her bookie $30,000. "I was just up last week, now I'm back in the hole with these fuckin bookies." She didn't want to admit it, but she had a bad gambling addiction. If she wasn't making bets with her bookie, Zikeema was in Atlantic City or Las Vegas at the blackjack tables. And if she wasn't in Atlantic City or Vegas, she was on the corner shooting dice with the fellas. All she did was gamble. Now she was in a bind and needed money fast.

"I need to call Stori and see if we can set up a job or something," Zikeema thought. She regretted having to call her sister. Zikeema didn't want to have to hear all the questions about how she didn't have money and how she should be saving. But she couldn't think of another way to make some big money fast. Most people thought Stori was older than Zikeema by the way Stori lectured her, but Stori was actually two years younger. Even when they were kids, it always seemed like Stori was maturing faster than Zikeema. As adults both Zikeema and Stori felt as if things haven't changed much from when they were kids. Now Zikeema was in a jam. She had to once again run to her younger sister for help.

Zikeema hid her gambling addiction from all her sisters. She felt that it was none of their business. She also didn't want to hear all the lectures again. After her class she needed something to do to rid the stress. "I know…let me call Ishmael, so I can relieve some stress." Zikeema thought about her on-again/off-again boyfriend. "Umm, that boy sure know how to lay that pipe." She thought. She pulled out her cell phone and dialed his number.

"Hello, who dis?" Ishmael asked.

"Is that how you answer a phone?"

"Damn girl, where you been? You was supposed to meet me at my house yesterday, what you forgot?" Ishmael asked, still a little mad he got stood up for the thousandth time.

"I'm sorry baby. I got caught up studying for my final that's coming up," Zikeema lied.

The truth was that she got caught up in a spades game where she lost $1,250.

"I can respect that. You know I be missing you though." Ishmael said, tired of Zikeema's excuses.

Ishmael was truly in love with Zikeema but lately he wasn't sure if the feelings were mutual. They've messed with each other on and off for the past five years. He wanted to marry Zikeema, but he was tired of all the games she played. Ishmael was one of the few that got rich from the drug game, but he got out before getting killed or locked up. Now he was successful in real estate. He sold and rented various properties. Nearly every single woman in the city and even a few married women wanted Ishmael to themselves, but all he wanted, or could think about, was Zikeema. Although he's been fed up with her lately, Ishmael knew he loved Zikeema unconditionally. The only thing was the excuses that she would always give. The excuses were running thin and Ishmael was tired of her shenanigans.

"I miss you too Daddy, that's why I wanted to come over right now. Are you home?" Zikeema asked in the baby voice that Ishmael couldn't resist.

16

"I should be home in twenty minutes. I had to check on one of my duplexes down West Philly, so meet at my house." Ishmael explained, excitedly.

"Okay, daddy. If you get there before me run some bath water for me. You know how I like it, nice and hot."

"Can I get in with you?" Ishmael asked, wanting to feel Zikeema's sweet lovin as soon as possible.

"Boy if you get in we ain't gonna never get out that tub."

"That sounds good to me," Ishmael said with a semi-erection. He started driving a little faster.

"I do miss Roscoe. I just want to kiss all over him," Zikeema admitted, referring to Ishmael's manhood who she playfully named "Roscoe".

"Fuck twenty minutes...I'll be home in five minutes. Last one at the house is a rotten egg." Ishmael hung up the phone pushed his Mercedes Benz SL 600 to the limit.

Zikeema quickly jumped into her Range Rover 4.6 and headed towards Ishmael's house to give Ishmael all her love. She knew she needed to treat Ishmael better before she lost him for good. That was the last thing she wanted. She loved Ishmael. She just didn't love him more than gambling.

Zikeema approached 16th Street and Susquehanna Avenue which was near Ishmael's house. She was listening to the song *Emotional* by Carl Thomas and saw a dice game going on at the nearby playground. Once she saw all the Benzes, BMWs, and Lexuses lined up, she knew money was there. She pulled up behind Squeak's Porsche, a Carrera GT, and figured it had to be over $100,000 in the crap game. Squeak was a major heroin dealer Zikeema and her sisters grew up with in the Hunting Park section of North Philly. Squeak had an endless supply of money and Zikeema wanted a piece of it. With her Dolce and Gabbana shirt and jeans on and her Manolo Blahnic shoe boots, Zikeema stepped out of her Range Rover. She put on her Versace sunglasses and headed towards the crap game with her last $6,500 in her Fendi bag. She stepped up on the crap game forgetting all about Ishmael. She hoped she could get a hot hand, so she could make back that $30,000.

CHAPTER 3

"Uwwww, baby don't you got to get ready for work?" Tori asked her husband Jerome, as he started playing with all her sensitive spots.

"I got time for a quickie. You know every time I get a quickie, I have a good day at work," Jerome said, sliding Tori's erect nipple into his mouth. Tori reached down to massage Jerome's morning erection.

"Ummm, baby stop teasing me and stick it in."

"Say please," Jerome said, as he started sucking on Tori's other nipple.

"Please baby…please don't make me beg," Tori said, as she squeezed even harder on Jerome's manhood.

Jerome straddled Tori and placed the back of her legs on his shoulders, as he kissed the insides of Tori's thighs. He slid 6 inches into Tori's love nest, holding back the other 4 inches he owned. "Baby, stick it all the way in," Tori begged while reaching around Jerome grabbing both his butt cheeks. Jerome finally slid all ten inches inside his wife. Tori let out a long moan. Holding each other tight, Jerome thrusted in and out of Tori with long slow circular strokes. Enjoying the warmth and wetness of Tori's love nest, Jerome took his time wanting to last as long as possible. After a few minutes of Tori's legs on his shoulders, Jerome pulled out and Tori flipped him over on his back. Tori climbed on top directing his manhood inside her. The thickness of Jerome's penis filled up every inch of Tori's insides.

She bounced up and down enjoying the ride. Jerome switched positions again laying Tori flat on her stomach as he entered her vagina from the back.

"Damn baby you hittin my G-spot," Tori said, biting into the pillow.

"I'm about to cum baby," Jerome said, as his inward thrust started getting deeper.

"Let's cum together baby," Tori said looking back over her shoulder as she gyrated her hips up under her husband.

"Daddy, what are you doin to mommy?"

Five year old Jerome, Jr. asked after busting inside of Jerome and Tori's bedroom and killing their oncoming orgasms.

"J.J., what did I tell you about walking into our room without knocking first?" Tori asked her son, pulling the covers over her and Jerome's naked bodies.

"I sorry mommy, but me, Lady, and Chewy are hungry," J.J. moaned.

"Ok, I'll be down in a minute to cook breakfast. Right now, take your brother and sister downstairs to watch T.V." Tori said, ready to finish what her husband started.

"Ok mommy, but Daddy…what are you doin to mommy?" J.J. asked again as his curiosity started to get the best of him.

"We just wrestling, that's all."

"I wanna wessle," J.J. said, running and jumping up on the bed. "Wessle, wessle," Lady and Chewy screamed as they ran into the bedroom.

Before Tori or Jerome could do anything, their kids were on the bed, jumping on their dad's back and wrestling with each other. When they finally managed to get all of the kids out of the room, it was time for Jerome to get ready for work.

"I'm a have to put in some overtime, so you and I can take a vacation." Jerome said while putting on his robe.

Tori just smiled at her husband as she started to feel guilty about her secret life. It killed Tori inside seeing her husband work so hard as a janitor at a local high school. He put in all the extra overtime he could so that his family could live a comfortable life. Tori felt bad seeing her husband work so hard when he didn't have to. If she could only tell him her secret, he wouldn't have to work so hard. Tori laid in bed in deep thought until she heard Jerome singing in the shower, breaking her trance.

"Let me get up and cook for my babies," Tori thought, throwing on one of Jerome's t-shirts and a pair of his boxers.

"Baby are you going to have time to eat?" Tori asked Jerome as she stuck her head in the bathroom.

"Naw, I'll just eat something at work," Jerome said, turning off the shower.

"Ok, I'll be downstairs cooking with the kids."

"Aight, but we got to finish up what we started tonight." Jerome said, grabbing his towel.

"Baby, I'm two steps ahead of you," Tori admitted with a devilish grin on her face.

Halfway down the steps Tori could smell turkey bacon cooking.

"I'm a kill this boy." Tori rushed down to the kitchen, ready to strangle J.J. for trying to cook.

When Tori came into the kitchen she found her identical twin Stori in there cooking.

"Girl you almost got J.J. killed, what are you doin in here?"

"What it look like?...I'm cooking for my niece and nephews," Stori said, standing at the stove with a blue and white Rocawear sweat suit on and a pair of all white Air Force Ones.

"What your ass doin up this early in the morning? You don't get out the bed til at least 12 noon." Tori said, leaning up against the kitchen counter.

"I woke up feeling good this morning. That and I had to pick up the rent money, from my hair salons." Stori explained, flipping over the turkey bacon.

"See, I knew you being up this early had something to do

with money."

Tori grabbed three glasses and three cups out of the cabinet and started filling them with orange juice.

"You know the only thing that makes me happy is making my own money and lot's of it." Stori bragged, as she tapped the bulges in her pockets.

"Money can't buy you happiness…you need a man."

"There's not a man out here on my level. After a week wit em, I get bored. So I dump his ass to the curb and let the next man entertain me for a week." Stori said with a big smile, showing off her pearly white teeth. "And you might be right about money can't buy me happiness, but it can buy me Gucci, Prada, Fendi, Chanel, Versace, Moschino, Dolce and Gabbana and anything else my little heart desires." Stori continued.

"Mark my words…somebody is gonna come along and be on a level a step above yours and you ain't gonna know what to do wit 'em." Tori said, grabbing the salt, pepper, and ketchup that was next to Stori.

"Whatever," Stori said coldly.

She rolled her eyes at her sister because she wasn't trying to hear Tori's logic.

"Aawww girl, you did that on purpose." Tori said as some of the turkey bacon grease popped onto her leg.

"My bad." Stori said with a slight smile.

"Don't get mad, because the truth hurts." Tori said, wiping the grease spot off her leg.

"The truth don't hurt like that hot grease, do it?" Stori said as they both erupted in laughter.

By the time Jerome came down stairs, breakfast was on the table.

"Hey, brother-in-law."

"What's up sis? When you get here?" Jerome asked, walking over to Stori and giving her a kiss on the cheek.

"I been here for a few minutes. I even cooked. You hungry?"

Stori waved her hands over the turkey bacon, cheese eggs, homefries, and wheat toast that was spread out on the table.

"Yeah…I am hungry, but I'm a have to grab something to eat at work, because I'm already running late." Jerome confessed, as he quickly drank down a glass of orange juice.

After giving his wife and kids kisses goodbye, Jerome was off to work.

"Come on, let's go sit in the living room while the kids finish eating." Tori suggested.

"Dang girl, you walkin all funny. What happen…Jerome was hittin dat from the back or something this morning?"

"Shit…I was trying to get my groove on, until your bad ass nephews and niece came barging into the room, interrupting my flow." Tori said, sitting down on the couch with here legs crossed Indian style.

"Leave my babies alone, you know they angels." Stori said, sitting on the opposite end of the couch.

"Please." Tori said as she grabbed the remote to the stereo turning it to WDAS 105.3, the local R&B station.

"Turn that up…that's my song right there," Stori said. Sade's song *Sweetest Taboo* came through the Bose speakers.

"Girl you didn't know nothing about Sade until I put you on to her."

"Whatever, just turn it up," Stori said, as she started singing along to the song.

Stori looked over and saw her twin sister in deep thought. "Damn girl, stop stressing…you'll get some more dick when your husband get home." Stori said, throwing a couch pillow at Tori.

"I'm not thinking about that. I'm thinking about all the money I got stashed while my soul mate gets up every morning bustin his ass at work, because he think we broke. Stori this shit is stressin' me out. Tori said, biting at her nails. I just wanna tell him so bad about my secret life, but I'm scared."

"Why don't you tell him you hit the lottery or something?"

Stori asked, picking food out her teeth with a straw.

"You know how many times I've used the 'I hit the lottery' story? After about the tenth time I told him that, he started getting suspicious. I got the kids college tuition saved and an additional $275,000 saved for me and Jerome's retirement. I figure if I can go with y'all on two or three more big jobs, I can save up enough to where I'll be comfortable. If I can save up a half a million or more...me, Jerome, and the kids will be secure."

"Well once you reach that half a mill, how you gonna hide that?"

"I'm not...I'm a confess all my sins to him and let him know I'm done. Hopefully he won't leave me, but I can't keep living my life keeping this secret from him." Tori said, twitching her nose, a nervous habit of hers.

"Look Tori, that man loves you to death, he ain't goin nowhere. He'll probably be mad at you for a little while, but he will definitely get over it."

"He better, cause I'm doin this for our future. Plus...like I said, after a couple more scores, I'm done for good."

"Well that's why I'm over here. Diamond put me on to some guy she saw at her booty shakin job." Stori said, gyrating her hips as she sat on the couch.

"That girl is crazy. All that money she got and she still dancing in them dirty ass titty bars. That girl need to find something else to do."

"You can't tell that girl nothing. As soon as you say something about her job, she gets real defensive. So I'm a leave it alone. But anyway, I've been following this guy for a couple weeks now. He owns a few bars, but he's selling more heroin than he is drinks."

"How do you know all this?"

Tori knew that ever since they were kids, Stori was always the mastermind out of all her sisters. She was always the one who found all the Christmas toys hidden in the house. Stori always had a plan to sneak out of the house without their Uncle Flea knowing, so they could go to a house party.

"I know all this, because I do my homework," Stori said, giving her twin a dumb look.

"My bad...please continue."

"Well his name is Shit-man and he's large," Stori said with excitement.

"Shit-man...what kind of name is that?"

"They call him that because every time something new comes out he's the first one to get it."

"I'm not quite following you."

"Ok, I'm a make it a little more simpler for you. Shit-man just bought the 2000 Bentley, and the year 2000 ain't even get here yet. After he bought it, he just rode around everywhere, shittin on the whole city. Therefore everybody calls him Shit-man, because he's always getting something new...shittin on everybody."

"Ohhh, now I get it." Tori said, leaning back on the couch.

"So anyway, he got a fat house, cars, jewelry, and I know he gotta have a big as safe in that big ass house of his. So I need you, me, Diamond, and Zikeema to meet up this week, so we can go over the plans."

"Just let me know when and hopefully when we're done, Zikeema can give me my money she owes me." Tori said, getting up off the couch to check on the kids.

"She owes you money too, what's goin on with that girl?" Stori asked, getting up off the couch with Tori.

"I don't know what's goin on with her, but I need my scratch. She had that shit too long." Tori said, pulling a wedgie out her butt.

"Ill girl...you nasty."

"Girl shut up and help me clean this kitchen."

"Shit I cooked. I'm not cleaning too."

Stori picked up her niece and walked back out of the kitchen with her nephews running right behind her.

CHAPTER 4

Emani was positioned on her hands and knees as Bobbi slowly entered Emani's vagina from the back. Emani closed her eyes and bit into the pillow, as all 12 inches of Bobbi's black penis entered her small built love tunnel. Bobbi wanted Emani to get as wet as possible. Once Emani's juices started to drip down her inner thigh, Bobbi pumped harder.

"Ohhh, Bobbi your going to split me wide open," Emani said, as her pain started to turn into pleasure.

"You want me to slow down?" Bobbi asked, looking down at Emani's golden brown heart shaped ass.

"No baby, I want you to go faster." Emani said, as she threw her heart shaped butt back on Bobbi's 12 inch penis. Bobbi quickly caught up to Emani's pace and started slamming her head into the cushioned headboard.

"Shit baby…smack my ass, I'm about to cum." Emani said with her eyes rolling into the back of her head.

Bobbi reached down onto the bed and grabbed a leather paddle. Bobbi then commenced to smack Emani's butt cheeks, leaving red marks, while Emani exploded with multiple orgasms.

"Who's pussy is this?" Bobbi asked, pumping and smacking Emani's butt harder and harder.

"This your pussy for life, can't nobody have this but you," Emani said, while looking over her shoulder back at Bobbi.

"This pussy better be mine." Bobbi said, reaching around Emani to massage her clitoris.

"Baby, let me ride you." Bobbi laid down. Emani got on top and started sliding up and down Bobbi's firm and solid 12 inches. Emani's feet were flat on the bed as she bounced rubbing on Bobbi's chest.

"Uhhmm, I'm about to cum again." Emani said, as she came harder then the first time. Emani fell onto Bobbi's chest drained of any energy she had left in her body.

"I love you so much." Emani said, while sucking on Bobbi's chest.

"No you don't," Bobbi said with an attitude.

"Come on Bobbi, we just got finished making passionate love that almost brought tears to my eyes. So please baby… don't start this."

Emani rolled off of Bobbi.

"What you mean don't start this? I'm tired of you keeping me a secret. Bobbi said, sitting up in the bed.

"You say you love me, but we have to creep around with each other. This is some bullshit."

"Come on Bobbi, I told you to give me some time."

"Give you some time…give you some time? We've been seeing each other for the past year and a half. How much time you need?"

Lost for words, Emani just laid on her back, looking up at the ceiling.

"Oh, now your going to give me the silent treatment? I don't believe this shit. When are you going to introduce me to your sisters?"

"Bobbi…in due time. Now isn't a good time for that." Emani said, rubbing her hands between Bobbi's legs, trying to get Bobbi's mind off the subject.

"Stop it Emani, we need to talk." Bobbi demanded, removing Emani's hand.

"Let's talk then."

"I'm saying, we've been in a committed relationship for a

year and a half, and you still want me to creep with you. If your ashamed of me, just say it because all this stringing along shit you trying to do with me got to stop."

"Baby don't think that. I'm not ashamed of you. I just need time to get my head straight. You know I got a lot on my plate right now. I love you and can't nothing ever change that," Emani said as she held onto Bobbi's hand.

"You love me? I can't tell."

"Bobbi, why can't we just lay in bed, make love all day, eat, make love again and just fall asleep in each other's arms?" Emani put on her baby face hoping that would be enough to make Bobbi drop the subject.

"You always try to change up the subject, when the subject is not to your liking, but I'm not dropping shit. We're going to lay everything out on the table, and hopefully we can come to some type of agreement. I love you too much to lose you, but I refuse to let you treat me like a stepchild, with no toes."

"Like a what...stepchild with no toes, huh? Bobbi you crazy, but baby please try to understand my situation. You know I'm trying to come along and be more open about our relationship. I just need to find the right words to say to my sisters."

"Oh, I forgot...the perfect Miss Emani Cooper has to show a good example to her baby sisters. Hold up, if I'm not mistaken... they're all fuckin grown."

Emani was the oldest of the five sisters. Ever since their mother died from breast cancer when Emani was eleven, she felt that she needed to take over the mother role for all her sisters and that's what she did. Cooking, cleaning, ironing clothes, helping them with homework, and everything else a mother would do for their child. Even now with all of her sisters grown and on their own Emani still plays the mother role. She always thought that she has to set the best example possible for her sisters.

Emani constantly kept an inconspicuous private life. She tries to set a good example for her sisters by working hard at her job.

Emani works at a prodigious law firm and has been gradually working her way to the top. She figures she could make partner in another five years. She would be the youngest partner and the first black woman the firm ever had.

Working as a criminal lawyer, she was highly recommended throughout the city. Emani loved doing pro bono work, never forgetting where she came from. Her professional life was in order, but her private life was a total mess. Bobbi wasn't making things easier for herself either. She loved Bobbi with all her heart. She was just afraid to find out what her sisters would think of Bobbi and what they would think of her.

"Well look, what's your perception on our relationship? Because I'm tired of walking around creeping with the woman I love and want to spend the rest of my life with."

"Bobbi please…I'm just not ready to share our relationship with everybody else." "Fuck this, I don't have to deal with this shit." Bobbi said, getting out of the bed with all 12 inches swinging.

"Wait Bobbi, sit back down and let me talk to you."

"I'm done Emani. Until you are ready to acknowledge our relationship and stop being ashamed of me, we're through."

Bobbi said as she took off her 12 inch strap on dildo, and threw it in the corner.

"You're gay. Just admit it," Bobbi added, as she walked towards the bathroom leaving Emani upset, confused, and crying on the bed.

CHAPTER 5

"Please Ziggy…just let me get one bag until later. I just need something to knock the edge off, before I get sick." Eddie Spaghetti pleaded. His eyes said it all, if he didn't get that bag of Heroin, he just might die.

"Get your dope fiend ass out my face. I fronted you a bag the other morning, because you said you was sick, and you still haven't paid me for that one." Ziggy said, giving Eddie Spaghetti a look of disgust.

"I promise you Ziggy, I'll pay you back…with interest," Eddie Spaghetti begged, as sweat poured off his face.

"How your broke ass gonna pay me some interest?"

"Please Ziggy help me out this one time." Eddie Spaghetti slipped his right hand in his pocket.

"Fuck you nigga, you are…"

"Yo Ziggy, give that mu'fucka a bag, so we can get da fuck out of here," Shit-man commanded.

"You lucky nigga, cause I wasn't gonna give you shit." Ziggy said, throwing the bag of heroin at Eddie Spaghetti's feet.

Eddie Spaghetti quickly picked up the bag of heroin and left. Ziggy walked to the car where Shit-man was sitting and got in. Ziggy had no idea that Shit-man just saved his life. Eddie Spaghetti had made up his mind. If Ziggy told him "no" one more time, Eddie Spaghetti was going to plunge the knife he had in his pocket into Ziggy's chest and take the dope.

"Damn Ziggy, why you playin games with the dope fiends?

You know we got business to take care of." Shit-man said when Ziggy got in the car.

"My bad Shit-man…these fiends be stressin' me the fuck out though. I swear I'm a fuck around and kill one of those mutha' fuckas one day." Ziggy said, as he leaned back in the Caravan's seat.

"Fuck them. Let's just handle this business, so we can get back."

Shit-man and Ziggy were headed to "The Badlands", a section of North Philly. Shit-man usually drove down by himself whenever he went to buy off his connect. One time when he went by himself to get a few kilos of heroin from his connect. When he came out, his car was gone. So every time after that he brought Ziggy along, so he could watch the car.

"How many bags you got left on you?" Shit-man asked Ziggy while pulling into traffic.

"I got seven left," Ziggy answered, grabbing the bags from his pockets.

Shit-man hit a secret button under the dashboard. A part of the floor on the passenger's side opened up revealing a secret compartment.

"Put them bags in there." Shit-man said.

Fifteen minutes later, Shit-man and Ziggy were riding through the "The Badlands".

"Damn Shit-man…you see all these dope fiends down here?" Ziggy asked.

"Yeah, it's dope city all down this bitch."

Shit-man drove pass the pet cemetery between 9th Street and Germantown Avenue where all the dope fiends got high. As Shit-man and Ziggy rode through the Badlands, all they could hear were drug dealers hollering out the name of their heroin. They would name their heroin to distinguish theirs from everybody else's. Names were used such as Polo, Fingers, Pac-Man, Chevy, Old Navy, Hot Water, Homicide, Bart Simpson, Super Buick and a host of others.

Shit-man finally pulled up to the corner of Cambria and Indiana and parked. "Stay in the car...I'll be right back,"

Shit-man walked toward a raggedy house with a bunch of kids playing out front. When Shit-man walked upon the steps one of the kids ran in the house and returned with an old lady.

"How you doin Momma-cita?" Shit-man asked.

"I'm fine Poppi...you're early, ain't you?" Momma-cita replied, as she turned and led the way into the house.

"Yeah...I'm ten minutes early. That's not a problem is it?" Shit-man asked looking at his Cartier watch.

"No, no...that's OK. Let's talk in the kitchen."

Shit-man followed Momma-cita through the house. In the livingroom was the same toothless guy he always saw sitting in his chair holding a double barrel shotgun. Shit-man wondered if the toothless guy ever left that chair. Shit-man walked past and gave the toothless guy a head nod. Just like always, the toothless guy just sat there giving Shit-man a cold menacing stare.

"Ya'll get ya'll asses out this kitchen and go outside and play." Momma-cita said to the six kids.

Once the last kid left the kitchen, Shit-man placed his book bag on the table and sat down in a chair. Momma-cita went to unlock the pad lock on one of the three old refrigerators she had in her cluttered little kitchen.

"Are you getting the usual?" Momma-cita asked, as she reached inside the old refrigerator. "Si Momma-cita," Shit-man said, practicing his Spanish.

Momma-cita pulled out five kilos of heroin and sat the brown bricks on the table.

"There's a slight increase on the price."

"How much?"

"Instead of 80, I'm a need 100." Momma-cita said, as she lit up a Camel cigarette.

"Momma-cita...are you kidding me? Instead of $80,000 you want $100,000 a key?" "Look, this just came straight off the boat from Africa. Nothing on the streets can fuck with its quality. Besides…this is from your motherland, no?"

"My motherland is South Philly where I was born and raised. I'm saying…a $100,000 a key is killin' me." Shit-man said furiously.

"I'm startin' to think that because I'm old you feel as though I'm a pushover. But you got me fucked up. So I'm a tell you like this. I don't like your attitude, so watch your tone. I'm not forcing you to buy my dope, cause once this shit hit the streets I'm not gonna be able to hold on to it. I figured I'd give you this diesel first since you are one of my good customers. But if you don't want to do business, you know where da front door is."

Momma-cita leaned back in the kitchen chair like an old gangster.

"Momma-cita, I didn't mean any disrespect. It's just…that's a little more than a slight increase. But if you say this will be the best shit on the street…I got to believe you."

"You know all I keep is the best, but this dope here is way better than the best." Momma-cita boasted, picking up one of the kilos.

"So what kind of cut can I put on it?" Shit-man asked.

"You can put a thirty on it and them dope heads out there gonna be noddin' so hard, they gonna be suckin their own dicks," Momma-cita said with a smile.

"I only brought the usual $400,000 with me, because I thought they would still be 80 a piece." Shit-man explained, tapping the bag of money that was sitting on top of the table.

"Poppi don't worry about it. Just bring me the $100,000 you owe me later." Momma-cita said, as she smashed a cockroach with her bare hands that had crawled up on the table.

Shit-man looked at the old Spanish woman and looked around the kitchen. He still couldn't believe how Momma-cita was living. All the money he gave her alone could buy Momma-cita a mansion with the works and that's not including the other customers she had. For some odd reason, Shit-man couldn't understand why Momma-cita chose to live in the ghetto. She lived in the middle of the notorious "Badlands" in a runned down house. Momma-cita seemed like a head turner in her prime. Now she was like the little old lady who lived in a shoe with all the kids running around the house.

"It got's to be about a thousand of these little bad ass kids runnin wild in the house". Shit-man thought, as Momma-cita pulled out her money machine.

Shit-man had been doing business with Momma-cita for the past four years and never once did he ever come up short with her money. Momma-cita still counted every dime before she handed over her work. Shit-man respected that because he knew you couldn't even trust your own mother in the game.

Shit-man quickly pulled out the neatly stacked bundles of one hundred dollar bills and slid them over to Momma-cita. After twenty minutes passed, Momma-cita was finished counting. "Yup...$400,000 on the dot." Momma-cita said, picking up her cigarette from the ashtray.

Shit-man wanted to ask her, "What else did she expect," but he just sat back and smiled.

"Jose come in here and put this up," Momma-cita shouted.

A boy, about 13-years-old, came in, got the money, and left back out the kitchen. Shit-man couldn't help but wonder what Momma-cita's stash looked like. He knew she had to have money up to the ceiling because he couldn't see what she was spending it on.

"Here you go Poppi and mark my words...once this hits the streets your workers won't be able to get no sleep cause the dope fiends will be up all day and night wanting this shit."

Momma-cita pushed the five kilos of heroin over to Shit-man who quickly stuffed the beautiful brown heroin into his bag.

"Well Momma-cita it's been a pleasure and as soon as I get up the $100,000 I owe you, I'll bring it straight down," Shit-man said, tossing the bag of heroin over his shoulder.

"OK Poppi, I'll be here."

Momma-cita walked Shit-man out. He walked through the livingroom and was once again met by the stare of the toothless guy sitting in the chair with his shotgun. Shit-man ignored the toothless guy and walked out the house. Taking a quick glance around to survey his surroundings, he felt the coast was clear and headed towards his car.

"Damn, Shit-man, I thought I might have to run up in there and come and get you. You was taking so long."

"Yeah...she up the price on me, so there's gonna be some pay cuts taking place." Shit-man said as he hit the secret button securing the five kilos.

"What you mean by a pay cut?" Ziggy asked, hoping that the pay cuts would not affect him.

"Don't worry bout it right now, will talk about it later," Shit-man said.

"Yeah aight," Ziggy said as he sat back in his chair.

"I already got the Quinine at the stash crib, for ya'll to cut the dope wit. You still got the coffee grinder right?" Shit-man asked Ziggy.

"Yeah."

"Good...Momma-cita said we can put a thirty on this, so just cut one brick for now," Shit man instructed.

"You sure all you wanna cut is one brick?"

"Yeah...just do one for now, so we can see how it moves. I don't want ya'll cuttin' everything and we end up sittin on the work...and da shit goes bad." Shit-man remembered learning the hard way. That if you cut the heroin all at once, and you don't move it fast enough, it will go bad.

"Aight I got you." Ziggy said with the pay cut still in the back of his mind.

"Good...now let's hurry up and get this shit out on the streets. So I can see if Momma-cita was telling the truth 'bout this diesel from Africa."

CHAPTER 6

"Everybody knows what they got to do right?" Stori asked Zikeema, Diamond, and Tori as they all sat around the table.

"Yeah we know," they all said in union.

"Everybody do as I say and this will go smoother than butter. Now here Diamond, put this on." Stori said, giving Diamond a mini skirt that would fit a ten year old.

"I can't wear this, my period is on," Diamond said, throwing the mini-skirt to Tori.

"I can't wear it either. Jerome would kill me if he saw me coming out the house with this on, looking half naked."

"Jerome would kill you if he knew what you was gettin ready to do too." Diamond remarked.

"Shut up," Tori said to Diamond, rolling her eyes.

"Well, Zikeema you got to wear it," Stori said.

"Why can't you wear it?" Zikeema asked with her nose turned up.

"Because I'm the mastermind of all this, so if you don't want to wear it, you don't have to go," Stori said to Zikeema.

"Fine, give me the damn thing." Zikeema said, not wanting to miss the chance of making some money.

"Now that that's settled, let's get down to business. This guy Shit-man keeps a tight schedule. Every morning he goes running and returns to his house at 7:45 a.m. That gives us two hours to get over there and set up. Everybody knows the rules. If shit don't feel right, shoot first, ask questions later…got dat?" Stori asked like she did before every job.

"Yeah...we know." Diamond said.

They all checked their semi-automatic hand guns.

"Let's go then."

Stori, Diamond, and Tori jumped into a work van. Zikeema followed them in an old '79 Chevy Nova. When they got to Moorestown, New Jersey Zikeema parked on the road, a few feet away from Shit-man's house. Stori, Tori, and Diamond waited in the van further down the block. There were only five houses on the whole block and they were all spaced very far apart. This was the perfect cover for what the sisters were about to do.

"Do you see the houses on this block? I know this nigga in there sittin' on something heavy." Tori said, peeking out the side window of the van.

"I know...right? I'm guessing he got a least six figures up in there, probably more." Diamond said, sitting behind the steering wheel of the van.

"Whatever he got up in there, we taking all that shit. We in and out...no pussy footin' around." Stori said confidently. She was always professional when it came to a robbery.

"Stori, we've been doin this for a long time now and trust me, we know all the rules," Diamond replied.

"What did uncle Flea always tell us?" Stori asked.

"We know...you can never be too safe," Tori and Diamond said at the same time.

"OK then. That's why I'm always repeating myself. We can never be too safe." Stori said, putting on her black leather gloves.

"You think Zikeema is aight out there?" Tori asked, as she stuck a piece of Trident gum in her mouth. She chewed gum before every robbery.

"Yeah she's cool and as long as we are cool, we'll be in and out. Ya'll feel me?" Stori said, looking from Tori to Diamond and then back at Tori.

"Damn Stori, we all on the same page...just relax," Diamond

said agitated.

"Both of ya'll chill…look. Is that him coming up now?" Tori asked, pointing to a jogger running up the road.

"You know it." Diamond said, looking at Shit-man as he came into view.

Just like Stori said. At 7:45 a.m., Shit-man came running up the hill.

"Zikeema, here he comes, so get ready," Stori said over the walkie talkie she held in her left hand while her right hand looked through a pair of binoculars.

"I'm ready. Just make sure ya'll ready." Zikeema said into her walkie talkie.

Zikeema placed the walkie talkie in her bra and waited patiently to make her next move. The hood was up on the Chevy Nova and Zikeema was bent over looking at the engine. When Shit-man came running up the hill, all he saw was the bottom of Zikeema's golden brown butt cheeks. Wearing a too short miniskirt and a thong, Zikeema appeared as if she didn't have on any underwear.

Shit-man saw all this plus the red fuck me pumps matching the mini-skirt. He couldn't believe his eyes. Shit-man felt his manhood stiffen as he got closer to Zikeema's golden brown butt cheeks. He could not see the gun Zikeema held in her hand and the rubber Ronald Reagan mask she wore over her face. By running up from behind, all he could see was a woman bent under the car's hood. He was stuck on the shapely slightly muscular legs this unknown woman owned. He swore her fat round ass was calling his name.

"May I be of some kind of assistance?" Shit-man asked once he got behind Zikeema.

"Yes you may. I'm a fair person so I'm a give you two options. Give me your money or your life."

Zikeema turned around pointing her 17 shot glock into Shit-man's face. He was frozen with confusion and fear. Before Shit-man could say or do anything a van pulled up behind him. The sliding side door opened and two more masked robbers jumped out pointing their guns at him. Stori wore a hockey mask while Tori wore a wolfman's mask.

"Get da fuck in the van pussy, before you end up in an ambulance," Stori said, holding her .45 automatic hard against the side of Shit-man's ribs.

Shit-man was visibly shaken as three different guns pointed at him from all directions.

"Lay face down, put your hands on the top of your head, and cross your feet," Tori demanded as Shit-man got in the van and did what he was told.

"Please..don't kill me," Shit-man begged. He layed on his stomach in the back of the van.

"Mutha'fucka…did I tell you to talk. Shut da fuck up before my itchy trigger finger gets some exercise." Stori said.

Stori kicked Shit-man in the side, as she got in the van sliding the door closed behind her. Diamond wore the black and white mask from the movie *Scream*. She drove the van up to Shit-man's house. Zikeema shut the hood on the Nova and jumped in the car following the van up the long driveway to the mini mansion. Once they reached the mini mansion, Diamond stayed in the van looking out for unwanted visitors. Everybody else entered Shit-man's house.

"Who up in the crib?" Tori asked Shit-man, as she, Stori, Zikeema, and Shit-man stood in the foyer.

"No....nobody," Shit-man answered, scared to death.

"If you lyin, I'm killin' you and whoever else we find in here…hear me?" Stori said.

She pressed her gun against the back of Shit-man's head. Unable to speak, Shit-man just shook his head up and down. Walking through the foyer, they knew they were about to make a come up. The inside of the mini mansion was beautiful. Expensive art decorated the walls. Italian furniture sat in the living room. The floors were all marble. Plasma flat screen TV's hung on five different walls. The whole place was laid out.

"Strip mutha'fucka!" Stori commanded with her .45 aimed at Shit-man's chest.

"Wha...What you mean?" Shit-man said nervously.

"Umm, I was hoping this pussy gives me a reason to shoot his ass. Ya'll know I ain't shoot nobody in about a week." Stori said, looking back and forth at Tori and Zikeema waving her gun in the air.

"Wait, wait...I'm doin' it," Shit-man said quickly. He started taking off his shorts. He stripped down all the way to his tight brief underwear.

"Did I tell you to stop stripping?" Stori asked.

Shit-man slowly took off his underwear leaving him naked from head to toe.

"Damn, I see why you didn't want to take your drawers off. Ya'll see how little this nigga dick is?" Stori said, pointing at Shit-man's penis. They all laughed.

"Maybe he's nervous or cold...or something." Tori said, trying to hold her laugh in.

"It's so cute, and little." Zikeema said, talking in a baby's voice.

Shit-man stood there feeling even smaller than his penis.

"Wrap your arms around that pillar." Stori instructed, pointing at one of the two pillars standing just beyond the foyer.

Tori handcuffed Shit-man's arms around the pillar.

"Now you tell me what I want to hear and you'll live to make this money back. If I don't like what I hear, I'm a jam this gun up your ass and pull the trigger...and you definitely don't want that." Stori explained. "It's a slow agonizing death...trust me. Now, where's the safe at?"

"It's in my bedroom closet," Shit-man said with no hesitation.

"What's the combination?" Stori asked.

"It's 2-19-27," Shit-man answered as his bottom lip

quivered.

"That's good…and don't worry, as long as you're cooperating you'll be aight." Tori said.

She used her black leather gloves to pick up the victim's sweaty socks and stuffed them in his mouth.

"President Reagan, do you have that duct tape on you?" Stori asked Zikeema.

"Here you go Jason." Zikeema said looking at Stori wearing the infamous hockey mask from the movie, Friday the 13th.

After Stori taped up Shit-man's mouth real good, they all went into action.

"Wolfman, you hit the safe." Stori instructed Tori. "President Reagan, you go up stairs with her and check all the other rooms."

Zikeema took the steps that were along the right wall leading upstairs. Tori took the steps along the left wall. Tori walked into the master bedroom and went straight to the walk-in-closet. She moved clothes and shoe boxes to the side trying to find the safe. After a few minutes with no success Tori started to panic.

"Damn, I hope this nigga ain't lie," she thought. Tori didn't want to go downstairs and tell her twin there wasn't a safe. She knew Stori would shoot the guy with no questions asked. She didn't want that blood on her hands.

"Think Tori…" she thought. She leaned against the mirrored wall. When Tori leaned against the mirror, she swore she heard a click. Tori pushed her body off the mirror and it popped open revealing a huge safe. She smiled and pressed the buttons on the digital safe. When she hit the last number, there was a click. She pulled on the handle and the safe's door swung open. Tori quickly started filling up her trash bag with stacks of money and jewelry. Tori smiled again knowing this score would put her a lot closer to her goal. Zikeema was ransacking all the other rooms taking anything that was small and valuable. They had a rule not to take big stuff. If it didn't fit in the bag they didn't take it.

"Are you done?" Zikeema asked, walking into the master

bedroom.

"Yeah…I got something nice," Tori admitted, clutching her bag.

"Did you look through his drawers?" Zikeema asked.

"No, I went straight to the safe."

"Hold up, let me look through his shit right quick."

Zikeema opened up a wood chest that sat at the foot of Shitman's bed and found about twenty different types of guns.

"Dis what I'm talking bout, yah mean?"

Zikeema picked up a .50 caliber Desert Eagle handgun showing it to Tori. After loading up all the guns, Zikeema and Tori went back down stairs.

"What's taking ya'll so long?" Diamond asked Stori over the walkie talkies.

"We'll be out in a minute. Is everything cool out there?" Stori asked Diamond.

"Yeah…everything's good…just hurry ya'll asses up." Diamond answered.

Stori continued to go from room to room looking for anything valuable. Stori entered the kitchen and opened up the refrigerator wanting something to drink. The mask she wore had her hot and thirsty. She grabbed a bottle of spring water off the shelf and then looked through the entire refrigerator. When she opened the vegetable and fruit compartments, she found four kilos of heroin.

"You ready?" Tori asked Stori, as she and Zikeema walked in the kitchen.

"Look what I found in the fridge." Stori said, holding up the heroin.

"So…you know we not no drug dealers." Tori said, holding the bag of money.

"Fuck that, we can sell that shit wholesale. Don't you know a key of heroin can go for…$50,000 easy. I saw Squeak the other day when I was riding pass a crap game." Zikeema said, telling half the truth. "I know he'll buy that poison."

"OK, let's go then," Stori said.

She placed the heroin in a bag and grabbed her spring water and walked toward the front door with Tori and Zikeema.

"We surely appreciate this." Tori said to Shit-man as she walked past him.

"Yeah mister, you're the greatest." Zikeema said, as she kissed the duct tape that covered Shit-man's mouth.

"I appreciate you not making me have to kill you, but don't get discouraged over this. Go on out there and get back on your grind, so we can rob you again…yah mean?" Stori said, smacking Shit-man on his bare butt cheek as hard as she could.

The smack stung so much it brought tears to Shit-man's eyes. Zikeema jumped back in the Nova. Everybody else rode in the van.

"Let's get out of here so we can count this paper," Stori said.

Diamond pulled off headed back to Philly.

CHAPTER 7

"You ready to handle your business?" Flea asked Becky.

"Honey, you know I'm always ready to handle my business." Becky said with a smile.

Becky and Flea walked into an expensive jewelry store in the Franklin Mills Mall. They both were confident they would get what they wanted. Flea, who walks with a cane, limped in the store wearing a three piece Giorgio Armani suit. He had a pair of alligator shoes that matched his suit perfectly. With his Gucci sunglasses and his Breitling watch covered with Diamonds, Flea looked like a million bucks.

Becky was one of Flea's many white women. She looked like she was straight out of Hollywood. She had blonde hair and blue eyes. Becky carried herself like some rich white man's daughter. She wore a DKNY business suit with a pair of high heeled shoes from Nine West. When they reached the store they knew exactly what to get. Flea and Becky wanted this to be an in and out affair.

"May I help you?" One of the white salesmen asked Becky.

"Yes, may I see this watch right here?" Becky responded pointing at a Movado watch.

The salesman took the watch out of the glass case handing it to Becky.

"Do you like this honey?" Becky asked Flea as she held the watch out to him.

"It's beautiful," Flea said. He leaned over looking at the watch but not touching it.

"I think this will look good on you," Becky said, placing the watch back on the counter. "This is one magnificent watch." The salesman said badly wanting the commission from the sale.

"Can I also see that bracelet?" Becky asked pointing at a bracelet in the display case.

The salesman pulled out the bracelet and immediately got into his sales pitch. "Yes, this is a beautiful piece of jewelry. These are two karat canary yellow diamonds set in platinum…"

"I'll take the bracelet and the watch," Becky interrupted, with an air of arrogance.

"Will that be cash or charge?" The salesman asked boxing and bagging up the two items.

"Charge."

Becky handed the salesman a Platinum credit card. The salesman ran Becky's credit card through the machine never asking for any I.D.

"Thank you for shopping with us," the salesman said handing Becky the bag with her watch and bracelet inside.

Then he handed Becky her Platinum card back with a $8,998 receipt.

"You're welcome. I'll be sure to tell my friends about your store." Becky said politely. "Good job baby…good job," Flea said to Becky as they walked out the store.

"I want my reward tonight in bed." Becky said, trying hard to switch her flat butt back and forth.

"Baby you know I got that covered." Flea responded, placing his arm around Becky's waist.

Ever since Flea got shot twenty years ago it left him with a bad limp. Unable to no longer run, Flea gave up strong arming. Now he was the biggest con-man in the city. Flea's current hustle was credit card fraud. He had a flock of white women working the credit cards for him. His logic was that a white woman wouldn't get questioned and hassled by a salesperson. He also made sure everybody was dressed for success. Flea knew that a person's appearance carried a lot of weight. That's why Flea wanted his women walking into stores with a mean swagger and wearing $5,000 suits. In his opinion, the only thing the salesperson would see was dollar signs.

Becky was Flea's number one money maker. It took a while for him to teach her the ends and outs, but now she was a master in the counterfeiting game. They never spent a dime on anything. They went to the finest restaurants, eating and drinking for free. Everything from clothes, to gas, to toilet paper, they bought with the credit cards. Flea also dealt with cashiers checks, certified checks, instant credit, and a host of other scams. He had a female friend that worked in a hotel and she supplied Flea with an endless supply of credit card numbers, social security numbers, names, and everything he needed to add on to his riches. Flea always said, "The paper game is a beautiful thang." He was making a lot of money and didn't have to break a sweat doing it.

Many of his friends got into the drug game, which Flea never looked down on, he just knew it wasn't for him. Flea thought selling drugs was too much work and too risky, a big headache. So he chose to stay away from drug selling. Flea's life was going just like he wanted it to go. His only worries were his four nieces, Zikeema, Stori, Tori, and Diamond. Flea wished they would reconsider his offer and go into business with him. He worried everyday about them. He didn't worry too much about Emani because he knew she was doing the right thing with her life. But the rest of them were making Flea's hair more grey by the day. Flea kept the promise he made to his best friend Big Toe twenty years ago. He raised Big Toe's five daughters like they were his own.

Flea never had kids of his own but he raised the girls the best way he knew how. Flea dropped out of school when he was in eighth grade. The only thing Flea knew were the streets and that's what he taught Big Toe's daughters. He taught them how to shoot guns, what to look for in a sweet victim, set up a good robbery, and even how to pick pocket people. Flea schooled the girls on every hustle he knew. He regretted what he taught them now that he was older and wiser. He knew he had to get them out of the strong arming business before something bad happened. It would kill him if something happened to any of his nieces because they tried to rob somebody. Then he would have to kill the person who caused his nieces bodily harm.

Flea figured before it came to that, he would make it his business to talk his nieces into either leaving the streets alone completely or going into business with him. Even though he know his nieces where bull headed, especially Stori, he had to keep trying.

"So where to next, honey?" Becky asked.

"Girl...what you think? We goin to another mall. We ain't finish shopping." Flea said, pulling out the keys to his Jaguar XJ8.

CHAPTER 8

Everybody was jammed packed in Palmer's, the popular nightclub on 6th and Spring Garden Streets. Women had on next to nothing and the men tried their best to flaunt their money and jewelry. The night was a special night, because Philly rapper Skeam was in the building. He and his entourage were sitting in VIP celebrating Skeam going platinum in the first week of his album's release.

"Yo! goin platinum in one week got to be some kind of world record. You da fuckin man Skeam!" Dave said. Dave was one of the guys in Skeam's entourage. He was jocking hard making sure when all the money started flowing he wouldn't be left behind.

Skeam sat there in his Enyce sweatsuit sipping on a bottle of Cristal. Skeam was bored and would have rather been at home playing John Madden on his Playstation. Skeam was zoned out as he looked around at his entourage celebrating like they went Platinum. Skeam knew that if he wasn't a rapper and was only a bus driver or something, none of them would even mess with him.

"Oh well, that's part of the game I guess," Skeam thought.

Cut Throat, another famous Philly rapper, walked up with two of his homies from South Philly.

"Damn Akh, I thought you was here celebrating goin platinum. You lookin' like you just came from a funeral."

"Cutty...what up Akh? I ain't even see you walk up." Skeam

said, cracking a smile for the first time that night.

"Congratulations fam," Cut Throat said shaking Skeam's hand.

"Thanks Akhee".

"I see you got every dime in here up in VIP wit you"

"You ain't lyin' bout dat, cause they definitely up in here." Skeam said, staring at a girl who's thong was sticking out the top of her jeans.

"Why you lookin' all down then?"

"Naw, I'm good…I just wasn't really in the mood for all this. I just wanted to stay home and chill. But you know my squad just had to come out. So I'm basically just here for them, feel me?"

"Yeah Akh, I'm definitely feeling you on that one. You know sometimes you gotta sacrifice your happiness for everybody elses." Cut Throat said shrugging his shoulders.

"The price you gotta pay for being famous". Skeam said sipping on his bottle of Cristal.

"This shit is definitely crazy…but look, I'm not gonna hold you up. Plus, I'm 'bout to bounce up outta here. But yo…if you find time come through the studio tomorrow. I got this hot track. I know you gonna want to get on..yah mean?"

"Aight Cutty, I'll do that." Skeam said giving Cut Throat a pound before he walked off.

"Yo Skeam, who you fuckin' tonight, cause every ho over there tryin' to give you some pussy." Skeam's homie Redz said as he took a seat next to him.

"I ain't fuckin' none of them hood rats." Skeam replied leaning back in his chair.

"You sure, cause they wanna fuck you and the whole squad."

"Well ya'll go ahead and do ya'll thang…I'm cool." Skeam said, looking out into the crowd.

"Aight, let me know if you need mc to do something for you." Redz said as he turned to walk away.

"Hold up…you can do something for me. You see that girl out in the crowd right there with the black and white on?" Skeam said, pointing with his eyes stuck on the dark skinned beauty.

"Where?

'Nigga, right there by the bar." Skeam said, placing his arm around Redz shoulder and pointing towards the bar

"Oh yeah…I see her. She fine as shit."

"Well tell her fine ass I'm tryin' to meet her," Skeam said with his eyes glued to the mysterious chocolate beauty.

"Aight, I'll be right back." Redz said as he left in a hurry.

"I can't believe you talked me into coming here." Stori said to Zikeema and Diamond as they made their way through the packed crowd in Palmer's Nightclub.

"Shit girl, it's jumpin up in here." Zikeema said, talking over the loud music.

"And this jawn is packed wit some fine ass niggas, right?" Diamond said, looking around the club.

"That's the problem. Niggas think since it's packed in here they can cop a free feel off you." Stori said, sitting down at the bar. "I'm tellin' you, I'm a get a free feel and punch one of these niggas in the nuts. If they rub up on my ass."

"Stori, you're a party pooper. Come on Zikeema…let's go find some guys to dance with." Diamond said. She and Zikeema walked to the packed dance floor leaving Stori by herself.

"Excuse me shorty can I talk to you for a minute?" Redz asked Stori as he walked up beside her.

Stori looked up and saw a guy that was black and big as a gorilla with bloodshot red eyes. Redz had a face only a mother could love.

"I know this big ugly nigga ain't tryin' to get his crack on?" She thought. Stori looked the gorilla up and down.

"Shorty…can I holla for a minute?" Redz asked again leaning in closer.

Stori sat there thinking. "Why not amuse myself with the big gorilla." She thought, figuring she may get a laugh.

"What's up sexy?" Stori asked Redz as she batted her eye lashes at him.

"Look ma, my man tryin' to holla at you."

"What…your man tryin' to holla at me? What type of elementary shit is this?" Stori asked with a frown.

"Look ma…my man Skeam sent me over to get you. He up in the VIP." Redz said, expecting that Skeam's name would cause her to jump out of her seat.

"Who da fuck is Skeam? The president or something?" Stori asked. She knew who Skeam was but not at all impressed.

"Naw, he a famous rapper. My man a fuckin' star and he want you to come kick it wit' em." Redz replied, a little cocky as he scratched his scruffy beard.

"You must didn't get a good look at me, I'm the fuckin' star up in here." Stori said.

She held her arms out to her side showing off her black and white Moschino outfit that was fitting Stori's body like a glove. Redz stood there speechless surprised by Stori's aggressiveness.

"I see the cat got your tongue…so if you find it by the time you get back over to your boss…tell him if he wants to talk to me stop sending a messenger. It's a turn off!"

Stori turned her back to Redz and continued sipping on her Bahama Mama. Five minutes later Skeam and three bodyguards were walking through the crowd towards Stori.

"Is this seat taken?" Skeam asked Stori, sitting on the empty stool beside her.

"I don't know. Is it?" Stori asked, looking up at Skeam.

"How you doin? I'm Skeam. I apologize for sending my boy over to holla at you. I don't know what I was thinking." Skeam said with puppy dog eyes.

"Yeah, I don't know what you were thinking either," Stori said as she used her straw to play with the ice in her drink.

"You was right though on what you said." Skeam said as he

looked at Stori from head to toe.

"Oh yeah, what was I right about?" Stori asked.

"You are a star." A slight smile came across Stori's mouth. Is that a smile I see?" Skeam asked Stori as he tried to break down the wall she had built around her.

"Maybe."

"Well look...this might sound corny, but why don't you come over to the VIP section so I can get to know you a little better."

"You can get to know me right here." Stori said.

"I know, but it's kind of..."

"WHAT DA FUCK?" Stori shouted, cutting Skeam off in mid-sentence.

"Damn sis, I'm sorry." A guy on the other side of Stori said. He accidentally knocked over his drink spilling it on Stori's purse and her arm.

Stori picked up her Louis Vuitton bag shaking off the spilled liquor.

"Like I was saying...it's kind of crowded over here so we can go over to the VIP where it's a little more laid back." Skeam said, pointing towards the VIP section.

"Yeah, let's go before I hurt somebody." Stori said.

All the females that were already in the VIP section gave Stori dirty looks when they saw her walking in with Skeam. Stori returned the dirty looks not blinking once. Skeam and Stori settled in a more intimate area of the VIP section.

"Have a seat. Would you like something to drink?" Skeam asked, pulling out a bottle of Cristal from an ice bucket. "Naw... I'm good." Stori said, as she placed a stick of Double Mint gum into her mouth.

"I'm sorry...I didn't catch your name." Skeam said, pouring himself a glass of Cristal.

"That's because I didn't throw it at you yet." Stori replied, leaning back crossing her legs.

"That was a cute come back." Skeam said, smiling and shaking his head at Stori.

The more time Skeam spent with Stori, the more she intrigued him. Stori was different then all the other women. Now he finally found a woman that might give him a challenge and he was loving it.

Skeam wasn't used to girls playing hard to get. Even before the rap career, fame, and money, the females always loved Skeam. Standing at 6'2", Skeam was a solid 220 pounds. He had deep thick wavy hair, thick dark eye brows, and long eyelashes that curled up at the ends. His skin complexion was ebony brown and he had a model's face.

"I know what your name should be." Skeam said, looking in Stori's light brown eyes.

"Oh yeah…tell me what it should be."

"It should be Mrs. Skeam, of course."

"Ha, ha, ha…I like your confidence."

Actually she liked a whole lot more, but she never played easy to get. After Stori told Skeam her name they talked like they were old friends. Stori enjoyed their conversation, but the wheels in her brain were turning. Being the mastermind that she was, Stori was already plotting on how she would rob Skeam. She knew she could retire in Miami somewhere with Skeam's money.

"So when are you gonna let me take you out to dinner?" Skeam asked Stori.

"Here…take my number and we'll talk about it." Stori said. She picked up Skeam's cell phone from off the table and punched in her number.

"That's what's up." Skeam said, knowing he couldn't wait to use the number.

"So what you doin after this?"

"Oh shit…I forgot I came here with my peoples. Let me go find them."

"Let me walk you."

"Naw, I'm alright. Just give me a call when you can."

Stori walked out of VIP. Skeam watched Stori as she walked off.

"Damn girl, where you been at? We were all on the second and third floor looking for you. We thought your ass left us." Diamond said.

"Naw, I was up in VIP...chillin."

"Stori, who was you up in VIP with?" Zikeema asked, sipping on her glass of Moet.

"That nigga Skeam came over here sweatin me." Stori said nonchalantly.

"You talkin 'bout the rapper Skeam?" Diamond asked with excitement.

"Yup...that's the one." Stori said, feeling herself.

"Yeah...what was he talkin about?" Zikeema asked, calculating in her head how much money Skeam had.

"He was trying to get his mack on, but of course I was playing hard to get. I just wanted to make him work a lil bit. Stori said smiling.

"Well Ms. Mastermind, what you think? Is he sweet or what?" Diamond asked.

"I can't tell yet, but I'm definitely gonna find out."

CHAPTER 9

Pop-pop-pop-pop-pop-pop-pop-pop-pop-pop-pop!
Tori held the gun in both her hands. Her feet were shoulder width apart as she emptied the clip into the paper target at the firing range.

"I told you I could make ten head shots. So give me my money." Tori said.

She held out her hand as Flea checked the paper target making sure that the guy on the paper had ten holes in his head and face.

"You always was the best shooter out of all your sisters." Flea said, pulling out a hundred dollar bill from his pocket.

"Thanks Unc." Tori said. She held the hundred dollar bill up to the light.

"What…you don't trust your Uncle Flea?"

"I remember the last time you gave me some money…it was counterfeit." Tori said, stuffing the hundred dollar bill in her pocket.

"I told you I dug into the wrong pocket." Flea said with his honest boy scout look.

"Well, I'm just making sure you didn't dig into the wrong pocket this time," Tori said, giving Flea a kiss on the cheek.

"So how's the family?"

"The kids are bad as ever and Jerome is still working hard to the bone," Tori said, with a frown on her face.

"I think you should just tell him you got a safe full of money,"

Flea said, loading up his gun.

"Easier said than done. I know if I tell him, I'll hurt him deeply. I'm not ready to do that."

"You know…you remind me so much of your mother. She always catered to everybody else's feelings before she catered to her own. She was the most caring person I've ever met in my life. I always smile to myself when you and Stori are together. Even though ya'll look identically alike, ya'll are total opposites. I always said, you were your mother's child and Stori was your dad's child."

Flea smiled as he reminisced about the good ol' days.

"I miss 'em both so much," Tori said.

"Yeah…me too. I just hope your mom and dad is not looking down mad at me on the way I raised you and your sisters. I mean I went from having no kids to raising five little girls. Shit…I wasn't raised right myself. So I raised ya'll the best way I knew how. Now that I look back on everything, I would of did things different. Now don't get me wrong, there's not a day that goes by that I ever regretted raising ya'll girls. You and your sisters are my life. If I had to raise ya'll over again a thousand times, I would do it without a second thought. I just would of raised ya'll different. I would of raised ya'll the right way."

Flea slid the fully loaded clip back in his gun.

"Uncle Flea, don't ever think you did a bad job on raising us. If you didn't take us in, me and my sisters would've probably grew up in separate homes. You kept the family together and you did a good job raising us. Look at Emani, she's the top lawyer in the city. Zikeema, she's in med school right now at Temple University. Stori, she's successful in the real-estate business. Diamond, well let's just say she's finding herself right now and as far as me…I'm nominating myself for being the best mother and housewife in Philly. So Uncle Flea, as you can see, you raised five strong independent females that's not on WIC or welfare. It's not your fault why we do what we do. It's just in our blood to duct tape and rob niggas. I truly believe we were going to rob people if you taught us the trade or not. So instead of focusing on the negative stuff we do, take a look at all the positive stuff we got going on in our lives. That should put a big smile on your face."

Flea leaned back and realized he never looked at it that way. He always focused on the negativity. He never found time to look at all the positive qualities of his nieces. Flea realized that their positives outweighed the negative things they did. That made Flea feel good.

"Is that a smile I see on your face?" Tori asked Flea.

"Yes it is and you know I am proud of you and your sisters. I couldn't ask for a better bunch of nieces." Flea said, giving Tori a hug.

"I love you Uncle Flea."

"I love ya back," Flea said, kissing Tori on her forehead.

"So what have you and your sisters been up to lately?" Flea asked.

"Same ol' thang. We robbed a guy over in Jersey a few weeks ago. We got 'em for a stash of money, and some drugs and jewelry, which we sold. We ended up getting $80,000 a piece after breaking everything down. Not bad for a 15 minute job, huh?"

Tori knew that even though their Uncle Flea showed them the art of strong arming, he still wasn't comfortable with them doing it. Tori just could never lie to her Uncle Flea.

"A $320,000 come up ain't bad. It's life threatening though. Imagine the guy pulled a gun or something and killed one of ya'll. Then I would have to kill him, his momma, his pops, grandma, uncles, dog, cat, goldfish and everybody else that nigga had love for. That's why ya'll should come into business with me. I'm tellin' you it's sweet. You make nice money and you don't have to worry about someone pulling a gun on you."

"I'm cool Unc, I'll be done with everything in a minute. One or two more jobs and I'll retire from the stick-up game for good."

Tori explained.

"I hope so, because I heard it before. One or two more jobs can turn into nine or ten more. I even talked to Stori the other day about giving up on stick-ups and coming into business with me. She tells me she loves the stick-ups because of the adrenalin rush. Can you believe her...just like your father. I tried telling her about the adrenalin rush you get playing wit dat paper and plastic, but she wasn't trying to hear it. Once again, your father was the same way. If he had it in his head he wanted to do it this way and not that way...there was no changing his mind."

"You know you can't tell that girl nothing, but as far as me, I got kids to think about. I'm only doing this so I can be sure their futures are secure. After that, I'll be your normal housewife and soccer mom. I wanna be around to see my babies have babies. I don't want to be dead or sitting in someone's jail."

"I'm glad you are thinking the way you are. Them babies need you alive, not dead and being in someone's jail. Being away from your kids gonna make you feel that you was better off dead anyway. Do what you gotta do and get out before it's too late."

"Unc...I'm on point, I know I can't do this forever. I still don't believe I've been jammin people for this long. It's just every time I think I'm going to retire, something comes up and I have to go into my stash again."

"Stop thinking you have to do everything on your own. If something comes up with the kids, the house, or whatever, instead of going into your stash call me and I'll give you the money. I'll do whatever I have to do to get you and your sisters out the stick-up game. So the next time something comes up stay out your stash and I'll handle it."

"OK Unc, I promise to leave my stash alone and get out the game as soon as possible," Tori said as she used her finger to cross her heart.

"Good, now if we can only get Stori, Zikeema, and Diamond

on point, everything would be lovely. So how's Emani doin? I can never seem to catch her." Flea said.

"Who Momma II?" Momma II was the name Tori and her sisters affectionately called Emani.

"Yeah Momma II."

"She's a workaholic, but she aight. I haven't seen her in a few weeks, but she does call me every other day. I swear that girl need a man in her life." Tori said, not knowing that a man was the farthest thing on Emani's mind. "Maybe she wouldn't be working so hard."

"You know, I was thinking about all of us taking a vacation somewhere together. Jaimaca, Bermuda, Aruba, Brazil, wherever ya'll wanna go, my treat." Flea suggested.

"That sounds like a good idea. I can't remember when we all took a family vacation together," Tori said excited.

"I'll get with everybody else and see if we all can agree on some kind of date."

"I just hope Jerome agrees to this. Him and I definitely need a vacation away from them Bey-Bey kids. But you know his pride is something else. If he knows you are paying for everything, he's not gonna want that hand out."

"Look, don't worry about that. I'll talk to him. Being a man, I know how our pride can get in the way. I'll think of something where he won't feel as though he's getting a handout."

"That's great…because a get away for Jerome and I will do us good. Them kids be driving us crazy. Do you know I found a gray hair in my head last week?" Tori said, stroking her long hair.

"I know your not complaining about one gray hair. Who you think gave me all these gray hairs?" Flea asked, rubbing his hand over his salt and pepper hair.

"Who? Because I know it wasn't me." Tori said with an innocent look.

"Don't give me that look. You and your sisters got my hair

getting grayer by the day. So it's just coming back on you with your kids." Flea said, with a big smile on his face.

"Yeah, yeah…you like that don't you?" Tori said, with her hands on her hips.

"Now you feel my pain," Flea said as he lightly pinched Tori's cheek.

"Sssstt, get away from me," Tori said sucking her teeth as her and Flea broke out laughing.

"You know I love you right?" Flea said, placing his arm around Tori's shoulders.

"I love you too Unc."

"Now, let's get back to the business at hand. I got double to nothin that you won't hit that target 10 times in the head again."

"You know you ready to go broke messin with me, but if you like giving away your money, I'll take it. Just make sure it's none of that funny money you be trying to pass off."

Tori held both of her hands on her gun and took aim at the target. Flea stood to the side smiling at his niece.

CHAPTER 10

The Cherokee Strip Club, better known around Philly as The Kee, was jammed packed with hustlers with pockets full of money and strippers that were ready to turn those pockets into rabbit ears. When first entering The Kee the air smelled of stale cigarette smoke, weed, cheap body spray, and hot sweaty funky sex. All the lights were dimmed except on center stage. The Kee had only one rule, that there were no rules. As long as your money was right, anything goes. The majority of the strippers walked around butt naked enticing ballers to dig deep in their pockets. For a small fee, there were special rooms where the ballers could take the strippers. In these rooms strippers would perform every sex act imaginable. Many of the strippers that danced and had sex would make more money than your average drug dealer. There were a selected few that danced but didn't have sex with the customers. They still made nice money.

"You see that trifling ass bitch on stage sucking that boy's dick?" Alize' asked Diamond.

"Yeah, I see her nasty ass. She was on stage earlier smoking a cigarette with her pussy." Diamond said with at twisted upper lip.

"Umm, bitches will do anything for some coins," Alize' said, shaking her head.

"That's why these niggas got da game fucked up. Thinking everybody in here is willing to do anything for some money." Diamond said.

"You right about that. These niggas don't even want lap dances no more. The first thing they asking you is "you fuckin." I swear that shit makes me sick to my stomach. I be ready to kick them niggas in the nuts for asking me some shit like that." Alize' said, demonstrating how she would kick somebody in the nuts. Diamond stood to the side laughing.

"You crazy girl." Diamond said.

"Yeah...call me what you want, but I'm tired of these disrespectful niggas." Alize' said.

"Excuse me, can I steal you away for a minute?" A guy asked interrupting Diamond and Alize'.

He placed his hand on Diamond's elbow. Diamond looked at Alize' making sure she was all right before leaving.

"Girl go 'head. I'm a walk over here and get me a lap dance." Alize' said as she walked as nasty as she could towards a group of guys.

"So what may I be assistance of?" Diamond asked, showing off her deep-set dimples.

"What's your name?" the guy asked. He explored every inch of Diamond's body.

"My name is Temptation." Diamond answered, licking her full lips.

"That's a cute stage name. I'm Corey by the way."

"Well Corey, what's on your mind?" Diamond asked. She thought that if she'd met Corey anywhere else, outside of her job, that she would probably date him.

"I was wondering if I could get a dance or two," Corey said smoothly as he looked Diamond up and down with is light brown eyes.

Diamond wore a nurse's outfit. Her skirt didn't cover anything because her butt cheeks were hanging all out. She didn't wear anything under her nurse's jacket except two happy face stickers over her nipples. She completed her costume with a nurse's hat. The majority of the dancers walked around completely naked, but Diamond always kept her private parts covered. Diamond loved dancing for guys, but she felt that having her private parts uncovered was too degrading.

They found an empty chair. Diamond laid down her rules before she started dancing for Corey.

"No touching the breast or coochy," she commanded.

Diamond told Corey he could touch her butt because she loved getting her butt cheeks rubbed. Corey began to enjoy himself as Diamond danced seductively. Corey obeyed Diamonds every rule as he rubbed Diamond's voluptuous ass. After the tenth song Diamond and Corey had worked up a sweat.

"Temptation, I don't want you to take this the wrong way or anything, but are you datin?"

"Naw...I don't get down like dat, but thanks for the lap dances." Diamond responded.

She was mad because she was enjoying Corey's company until he spoiled it by asking for sex. Diamond got up, and walked away with the $500 Corey gave her.

"Dang girl, I thought ya'll was gonna get married over there." Alize' said, walking up to Diamond.

"Yeah...he was nice until he asked me was I datin."

"No that nigga didn't go there. See, what I tell you. These nasty bitches in here is fuckin da game up. These disease infected bitches fuckin for 40 and 50 dollars got all these niggas spoiled. Now they expect to get some pussy from all of us. I swear, I could stomp one of these dirty ho's in the ground."

Alize' was Diamond's partner in crime. In the go-go game, someone needed to watch your back and that's what Diamond and Alize' did for one another. Alize' had the same morals as Diamond. She danced for money but she wasn't having sex for money. It didn't matter how much a guy offered.

Just like Diamond Alize' was a beautiful woman. Alize' was petite and bowlegged. At 4 foot 11 inches tall, she looked more like a little girl than the grown woman she was. She had smooth light skin that complimented her grayish green eyes perfectly. Her butt was a perfect peach shape, and her breast sat up on her chest like two cantaloupes. The men in the club would gravitate around Alize' and Diamond, causing all the other go-go dancers to get mad. This always put a smile on Alize's face because she loved knowing the other girls in the club were jealous of her and Diamond.

"Fuck these ho's. They'll get what they got comin to 'em." Diamond said.

"What's up girl, ya'll hear about China?" Strawberry asked as she walked up on Diamond and Alize'.

"Naw, we ain't hear nothin. Why what happened?" Alize' asked Strawberry.

Diamond and Alize' occasionally entertained Strawberry's company only because she kept all the information on what was going on in the club.

"Girl, she went on a date last week and they ended up finding her in Fairmount Park." Strawberry explained. She was happy that she was the first to tell this information to Diamond and Alize'.

"She dead?" Alize' asked.

"No, but they said she's in a coma looking like she's half dead." Strawberry said, making sure she explained every detail.

Diamond and Alize gave each other looks that said "I told you so."

"Damn, I was wondering why China's money hungry ass wasn't here tonight." Alize' said.

"She fucked up bad huh?" Diamond asked Strawberry.

"Yeah…they said they're waiting for her to wake up, to see if she can identify her attacker." Strawberry said, acting like she worked for Channel 6 Action News.

"See, that's why I stay strapped," Diamond said, with a serious look on her face. "If one of these crazy ass niggas try to violate me, I'll put so much lead in 'em, they gonna be looking like a number 2 pencil."

"I hear that girl," Alize' said, giving Diamond a high five.

"Girl, I'll be back," Strawberry said. She spotted a group of strippers across the room.

Strawberry prayed that they didn't hear the news about China yet so that she could be the first to tell them.

"See…I told you some shit like that was gonna go down," Alize' said to Diamond.

"I don't want to sound cold, but fuck her. She brought that shit on herself." Diamond said.

"I know, I don't feel sorry for her either. She always thought her shit don't stink anyway." Alize' said.

"Uhhmmm, look at all those cute guys that just walked in. Hurry up and walk me to the dressing room so I can put this money up in my locker." Diamond said, with a serious look on her face. "I wanna get back out here so them guys can pay me for admiring my body."

"Here I come Miss Conceded, plus I need to put on some more lip gloss." Alize' said, following right behind Diamond.

"You see all the ice dem niggas had on? I know I'm a get paid tonight." Alize said, with intentions of taking every dime from the men in the club.

"I'm comin at the guy that's wearing…hold up, what da fuck are you doin' to my locker?" Diamond asked Precious who was prying back the door on Diamond's locker.

"Oh…dis your locker? I thought it was my locker. I was wondering why my combination wasn't working. Precious said, playing dumb.

"Bitch, you know this is not your locker. Your locker way da fuck down there." Diamond walked up to Precious so that they were standing face to face.

"Who you callin a bitch?" Precious asked stepping out of her high heels.

"You…you thievin' ass bitch", Diamond said in her boxer

stance.

"You think I'm a bitch? Put blood in my mouth and I'm a show you who da bitch is." Precious said trying to intimidate Diamond with her 6 foot, 190 pound frame.

Before Precious could react, Diamond was up in Precious' chest with hand speed that would make Sugar Ray Leonard proud. Diamond connected with a straight right jab and an over hand left. Both punches found their mark on Precious' mouth, splitting her bottom lip. Filled with rage, Precious awkwardly charged at Diamond, throwing wild punches. Diamond side stepped smoothly to her left allowing Precious to run head first into the wall. An embarrassed Precious turned around and charged Diamond again. Focused on Diamond, Precious never saw Alize' standing on the side with a metal folding chair in her hand. Coming from behind her, Alize' swung the chair and hit Precious with all her might. The blow caught Precious in her neck and back sending her to the floor in agony. Diamond picked up Precious' high heels and began beating Precious in the head and face. Alize' jumped off the bench landing on her as Precious laid spread out on the floor. Diamond brought back her foot as far as she could and kicked Precious in the head. The blow knocked Precious out cold.

"Oh shit, you hear this bitch? She fuckin snoring." Alize' said. Precious was curled up like a baby on the floor.

"Yeah...I put that stealin ass bitch to sleep and she was talking all that gangsta shit. Yeah, Bitch I put blood in your mouth, what you gonna do about it?" Diamond said, bending over Precious' sleeping body.

"Let's get da fuck out of here before somebody comes," Alize' suggested.

They started to leave the locker room after collecting their belongings.

"Alize', what the hell are you doin?" Diamond asked.

"Shit girl...I gotta pee," Alize' said. She lifted up her skirt, pulled her thong to the side, squatted over Precious' face, and started urinating.

"Ha, ha, ha, ha, ha…girl you is fuckin' crazy. I don't believe you doin that." Diamond said. She watched Alize' make faces like she drank a 40oz of beer and was holding her piss in all day. The urine splashed all over Precious as she slowly started to wake up.

"Girl, hand me some tissue." Alize' said, as her last bit of urine dripped onto Precious.

"Im not gonna ever forget this shit. You really crazy." Diamond said, handing Alize four baby wipes.

Alize' wiped herself from front to back and discarded the used baby wipes onto Precious' chest.

"Bitch go back to sleep." Alize' stomped on top of Precious' head so hard that it bounced off the cement floor three times.

"I hope we ain't kill da bitch," Diamond said, as they made their exit unnoticed.

"I never trusted that sneaky bitch," Alize' said.

"I knew the bitch was sheisty, but damn…she ain't have no look out or nothing." Diamond said, shaking her head. "The bitch is either bold or retarded as shit. Like nobody was gonna walk in on her."

"Fuck that bitch. She got what she deserved. I'm hungrier than a hostage though. You wanna go get some breakfast?" Alize' asked Diamond, as they stood outside in front of their cars.

"Naw girl, I just wanna go home and soak in the tub. My dogs are killin me." Diamond said, as she deactivated the alarm on her Mercedes Benz.

"Well I'm goin' somewhere to get me some fish and cheese-grits," Alize' said, climbing into her Ford Expedition.

"Aight crazy, I'll give you a call tomorrow," Diamond said laughing.

Diamond replayed in her mind what happened in the locker room. She got in her Benz and took the twenty-five minute drive to her home in Bala Cynwyd, a suburb of Philadelphia. Diamond pulled into her garage. The garage door closed behind her once she was all the way inside.

"Home Sweet Home," Diamond thought, ready to take a nice hot bath.

Diamond went straight to the bathroom. She grabbed her Victoria Secret bubble bath, adjusted the temperature of the water just the way she liked it, poured herself a glass of White Zinfandel, and then got undressed. Diamond turned on Toni Braxton's cd, lit her scented candles, and got in the tub. She laid her head on the small pillow in the back of the tub. Diamond then closed her eyes with no worries in the world.

*****

Meanwhile, Corey sat in his car in front of Diamond's house. She had no idea that Corey followed her after she left The Kee.

"I don't believe this bitch. I gave her $500 for lap dances and she wouldn't even go on a date with me. Fuck this, I'm a take me a date." Corey said to himself, as he stabbed the car's dashboard with a big Rambo knife.

CHAPTER 11

Zikeema collapsed onto Ishmael's chest after her fourth orgasm. Both of their sweaty bodies stuck together as they both breathed heavy trying to catch their breath.

"Ahhh…shit, get up! Get up!" Ishmael said as he threw Zikeema off of him.

"Boy, what da hell is wrong wit you?" Zikeema said. She grabbed onto the head- board of the bed, so she wouldn't hit the floor.

"I got a fuckin cramp in my leg. Ahhh…fuck, this shit is killin me." Ishmael shouted, grabbing his right leg.

"Aww baby, where it hurt at?"

"Right here," Ishmael said pointing to a real big lump in his leg.

"Watch out, let me see it," Zikeema said as she grabbed a bottle of baby oil off the dresser.

She poured the oil in her hands and started massaging the cramp out of Ishmael's leg. The cramp was gone after a few minutes.

"It feels better baby," Ishmael said as he slowly moved his leg up and down.

"Anything for my dukey butt," Zikeema said, kissing Ishmael on his lips. "Let's get in the shower. I'm sticky all over."

"Aight, we can do that," Ishmael said. He smacked Zikeema on her butt as she got up off the bed.

Ishmael and Zikeema got into the shower together. Forty-five minutes later, after making love again, they finally managed to get washed up.

"Let's get outta here. My skin is starting to look like a raisin." Zikeema said, looking at her fingertips.

"Don't you mean more like a prune?" Ishmael said smiling.

"Boy, shut up," Zikeema said, hitting Ishmael.

"Look...I gotta check on a few of my houses. Are you gonna stay here and wait for me to get back?" Ishmael asked Zikeema as they stood in the bedroom and dried each other off.

"I'm not going nowhere. I'm a lay naked across this bed until you get back so you can make love to me again." Zikeema replied as she grabbed her Victoria Secret pear scented lotion and placed it on the bed.

"Aight, I'll be back in about a half an hour," Ishmael said as he slid on his polo sweat pants.

"Eehhh, you not gonna put on no underwear?" Zikeema asked, frowning up her face.

"Nope, I'm goin' white boy style," Ishmael said, putting on his white t-shirt and all white Nike Air Max's.

"Bring something to eat back."

"What you want?" "Go to Sid Booker's and get some fried shrimps."

"Aight baby, I'll be right back." Ishmael said.

He kissed Zikeema on the lips and walked out the door. Zikeema laid naked across the bed with her lotioned body. She started to nod off when her cell phone rang.

"Hello." Zikeema said, snatching the phone with an attitude.

"Yo Keem, you gotta come through. These niggas holdin six figures down here," Damon announced.

"Down where?" Zikeema asked already putting on her clothes.

"I'm down here at Ol' Man Rusty's spot. These niggas shootin' dice. It ain't no mu'fuckin' spud game either. These niggas high rollers."

"I'm on my way", Zikeema said, hanging up.

Damon smiled knowing Zikeema would be there shortly. Zikeema and her sisters grew up with Damon, who was a neighborhood friend. Damon could never figure out how the sisters made their money. He just knew that the sisters always had money to spend and as a close friend of the family, Damon would occasionally benefit from their generosity. Many thought that Damon had big money because of his clothes and jewelry. Damon was actually broke and living day to day, but Damon was able to make some extra money for himself by going around to different gambling spots. If big money was in the game he called Zikeema. Once Zikeema arrived at the game, if she won, she gave Damon a certain percentage of her winnings. In return Damon watched Zikeema's back. So if she won, they both won.

Damon was outside smoking a Newport cigarette when Zikeema pulled up. She jumped out of her Range Rover 4.6 wearing a pair of Parasuco jeans, a Polo shirt, some Prada sneakers, and a pair of Safilo's Burberry sunglasses.

"What's it hittin' for?" Zikeema asked, walking toward Damon.

"Keem, they in there bettin $1,500 on sixes & eights and they layin the shooter $4,000 to $2,000 on 4's and 10's," Damon explained, plucking ashes from his Newport cigarette.

"That's the numbers I wanna hear. Now lead the way to this money, I'm about to win", Zikeema said, following Damon into the house.

Damon and Zikeema entered the basement and were greeted by weed and cigarette smoke. The high rollers were talkin' shit real loud back and forth to each other. Ol' Man Rusty stood behind the bar where he sold and served alcohol. There were two groups of guys in the basement. One group shot dice on a pool table…A.C. style. The other group shot dice against a wall… street style.

"So, what game got da big money?" Zikeema asked, standing

between both games.

"All the high roller's over there," Damon said, pointing to the guys against the wall. "That's where I belong then," Zikeema said.

When Zikeema reached the dice game everything stopped moving. All the high rollers stared at Zikeema's beauty wondering who the dime piece was.

"What's the point?" Zikeema asked, breaking the ice.

All the high rollers looked around at each other. Until one of them finally told Zikeema the point was 8.

"I don't like your eight, bet $1,500," Zikeema said to the guy in the middle holding the dice in his hand.

"Shit…it's all good, put your money on the wood. I don't discriminate." The guy shooting the dice said. He then smacked the M.O.B. tattoo on his forearm, which stood for money over bitches.

The dice game went back and forth between all the high rollers. No one really got the upper hand. Their legs and backs were in pain from hours of bending over the crap game. Even with pain, the high rollers never took a break. The stakes were just too high. Zikeema finally got on the dice and got a hot hand.

"Little Joe owes me rent money," Zikeema said shooting the dice and hitting her point, which was a four.

"Pay a bitch," she yelled, collecting her money from all the side bets. "Yeah, this what I do right here." Zikeema bragged, taking count of the money she won making sure that it wasn't short.

"Is you gonna talk shit or shoot da dice?" asked one of the high rollers wearing an Akademik sweat suit.

"I'm a do both," Zikeema said, as she shot the dice. "9, what ya'll bettin?" Zikeema asked as a 5 and 4 showed up on the dice.

Everybody laid Zikeema $3,000 to her $2,000.

"That's what I'm talkin bout. Money on da wood right? Watch how I make Nina show her ass." Zikeema said as she schooled the dice.

"Damn..just shoot da fuckin' bones and stop talking shit," the guy in the Akademik sweatsuit said.

"I see you anxious to lose your money," Zikeema said as shot the dice. Her roll landed on a three and two.

"Uhm, you know Feva da indicator. Now where you find fish at? Right between Nina's legs." Zikeema said, shooting the dice and hitting the nine. "I'm about to close up shop in this bitch. I ain't break ya'll niggas yet?" Zikeema continued, stuffing money in every pocket she had available.

"This bitch loves talking shit, don't she?" The guy in the Akademik sweat suit said to no one in general.

"That's because this bitch can back it up," Zikeema answered. Damon stood to the side with his hand on his gun.

"Since you can back it up, bet everything you got on you," The guy in the Akademik sweat suit responded.

"Hold up Big Tyme, I'm tryin' to win some of my money back. You tryin' to make this shit personal and cut the rest of us out, or something?" Another dice shooter said who wore a Gucci sweat suit.

"Naw Jamar, I'm not trying to do no shit like that. I'm a break this bitch then we gonna finish shootin." Big Tyme said, staring at Zikeema.

"You not saying nothing but a word...bet that shit," Zikeema challenged.

"Ol' Man Rusty, here go $100. Let me see your money machine." Big Tyme said.

He handed Ol' Man Rusty a crisp brand new one hundred dollar bill. Ol' man Rusty gave Big Tyme a toothless smile then pulled out his money machine. Ol' Man Rusty would rent out his money machine. He knew getting that money machine was the best investment he ever made. Zikeema counted her money first. When the machine finished counting Zikeema had a total of $67,850.

"Can you cover dat?" Zikeema asked smiling.

She tried to cover her shock because she didn't realize she made that much money. Licking his lips, Big Tyme smiled and took off his sweat suit jacket. Under his jacket he wore a money suit. The suit fitted like spandex against his body. The money suit had pockets all over it that held stacks of money perfectly. Big Tyme pulled out seven stacks of money. Each stack held $10,000 all in 100 dollar bills.

"Yeah, I think I got dat covered," Big Tyme said placing the stacks of money on the table.

Zikeema's eyes got big after seeing all that money, making her greed take over.

"What, we gonna shoot one dice to see who rolls?" Zikeema suggested.

"Naw, you can roll and since we bettin straight up, pick your point...6 or 8."

"I'm a roll these box cars on your ass," Zikeema said, picking her point to be 8.

"Well stop flapping that pink thing in your mouth and roll da dice," Big Tyme said as he placed the dice on the table.

Zikeema took in a deep breath and exhaled. She then checked the dice making sure they weren't hooks. Hooks were loaded dice that were fixed to make you crap out. Zikeema didn't want to have to kill Big Tyme over loaded dice.

There was just too much money at stake. Everybody got quiet and focused on Zikeema. She felt like everything was in slow motion as she listened to the dice shake in her hand. Feeling confident, Zikeema threw the dice from her small hand. She stood up from her squat position and watched the two dice bounce towards the awaiting wall. The first dice stopped on a three. Zikeema's eyes got big. The second dice slid towards the wall with a 5 showing. Zikeema prematurely started to celebrate thinking she hit the eight. But when the second dice hit the wall it bounced off the 5 and landed on 4.

"Ohhh, that's my number right there. Give me my money." Big Tyme said, snatching up Zikeema's $67,850.

Zikeema stood there with her mouth open. She couldn't believe she jut lost $67,850 in a matter of seconds.

"I knew that mouth was gonna get you in trouble. Now look where it got you...I'm tellin' you, that mouth is probably only good for a mean dick suck." Big Tyme laughed as he counted his winnings in Zikeema's face.

"Pussy, what da fuck you say?" Zikeema snapped, She advanced towards Big Tyme with her fist balled up tight.

"If you feel froggy, leap," Big Tyme said, holding his ground.

Damon ran up before Zikeema reached Big Tyme, cutting her off. "Damon get out my way," Zikeema said furious.

"Naw, fuck that nigga. He ain't worth it." Damon said.

"Yeah homie, hold your girl before she get's herself in trouble," Big Tyme said to Damon.

"Fuck you pussy...matter fact, you gonna fuck around and have 18 people real mad at me," Zikeema said, biting her bottom lip."

"Eighteen people gonna be mad at you? What da fuck are you talking bout?" Big Tyme asked Zikeema, giving her a dumb look.

"The twelve people sittin in that jury box that's gonna be judging me, and the six people carrying your body at your funeral. All them mutha'fucka's gonna be mad at me if you keep runnin your mouth." Zikeema said, with a crazy look in her eyes.

"Wha...wha...whatever," Big Tyme said stuttering. All the other high rollers snickered in the background.

"Now come on ya'll, we ain't gonna be having that in here," Ol' Man Rusty said.

"Fuck you too old man," Zikeema said to Ol' Man Rusty. She left the gambling spot with Damon walking behind her.

"Keem, don't even worry about dat nut ass nigga," Damon said to Zikeema outside.

"I'm not worrying about it, cause I'm a get mine." Zikeema paced back and forth on the sidewalk.

"You know you will make that right back…early." Damon said, confident of Zikeema's ability to get money.

"Look, that nigga hit me for everything. But trust me, I'm a break you off with something sooner than you think." Zikeema said, plotting on her next move.

"Keem, I'm not worried bout dat. You know we like family. I just wanted to make sure you was aight."

"Yeah, I'm cool. I'm a just go back to the crib and chill. I'll call you later on though." Zikeema said sticking her fist out as Damon gave her a pound.

Zikeema walked towards her Range Rover. She watched Damon get into his Acura Legend and leave. Zikeema got into her Range Rover and reached under her driver's seat. She pulled out a gym bag and opened it. Inside was a black Dickie coverall jump suit, black gloves, a black ski mask, and black Timbs. Zikeema quickly placed everything on the passenger's side seat. She took off her Prada sneakers and placed them under her seat. She slid the Dickie coveralls on over her clothes. She then put on her Timbs and black leather gloves. Zikeema hit a secret button under her dashboard. She held the button in for ten seconds causing her back seat to pop open. Zikeema reached in the backseat and pulled out a black .50 caliber Desert Eagle handgun. The look of a Desert Eagle hand gun made the toughest men softer than drug store cotton. Zikeema sat behind her 35% tint she had on her truck's windows and waited. An hour and forty-five minutes had passed without Big Tyme leaving. Zikeema started having second thoughts. Then Big Tyme finally walked out.

"Oh fuck that, it's on," Zikeema said.

She watched Big Tyme jump in his red Mercedes Benz SL500 and pull off down the street. Cautiously, Zikeema followed the red Benz from a distance. Her Uncle Flea taught her and her sisters how to follow somebody without them having a slight hint that they were being followed. Zikeema followed Big Tyme to a quiet block in Yeadon, PA, a small town just outside of Philly. Big Tyme pulled into his driveway on the side of his house and turned off his Benz. Zikeema quickly parked five houses down and jumped out of her truck. Using the cover of darkness and ducking behind trees and bushes, Zikeema approached. Zikeema was like a hungry lioness as she stalked her prey. Big Tyme was lifting bags out of his trunk. His back faced the street.

"Nigga, give me a reason to pull this trigger," Zikeema said. She held her Desert Eagle steady against the back of Big Tyme's head. Big Tyme, frozen in fear, dropped his bags to the ground.

"I got money in my pockets. You can take that and my bags. Please, just spare my life. I got six kids." Big Tyme said with a shakey voice.

He also said a silent prayer asking God to get him out of this unharmed.

"I love da kids, so do as I say and they'll get a chance to spend another day wit they father...Now strip?"

Big Tyme slowly started taking off his clothes. He wished the person that was sticking him up would just take the money in his pockets and leave.

"If you don't move faster than what you movin, I'll be taking clothes off a dead body and don't make any sudden moves or I'll put two slugs in the back of your head." Zikeema said through gritted teeth. "Trust me...I don't miss."

Big Tyme quickened up his pace taking his sneakers, sweat pants, and sweat suit jacket off. Big Tyme stood there revealing his money suit. The money suit was filled with currency up and down his legs, chest, and arms. Money was neatly packed inside pockets all over the suit.

"Now you know that wasn't nice. You're not playin fair, trying to hold out on me. Take dat shit off before I split your muthafuckin wig to the light skin meat."

He unzipped and removed the money suit leaving only his

boxers and socks.

"Now climb inside your trunk," Zikeema ordered.

Big Tyme slowly climbed inside and laid sideways inside the spacious trunk of his Mercedes Benz.

"I hope you're not scared of the dark." Zikeema said just before closing Big Tyme inside the trunk of his Benz.

Quickly gathering everything, Zikeema put the clothes and money suit in the bags. She carried the bags back to her truck never looking back.

"Damn, I'm fuckin untouchable." She said to herself.

CHAPTER 12

"Emani! It's your shot." Diamond said for the third time.

They both were playing pool at Dave and Buster's on Delaware Avenue. Emani wasn't really into the game. Ever since her and Bobbi's break up, things haven't been the same for Emani. Once focused and unwavering, Emani now finds herself day dreaming all day. Day dreaming about Bobbi. Emani has been backed up on several cases for weeks. Bobbi wasn't making it any easier for Emani by not answering Emani's calls. Now Emani is trying to spend quality time with her sister, but Bobbi still flooded her thoughts. She wished she could confide in her sister about Bobbi.

Emani's love ran deep for Bobbi. She day dreamed often about her and Bobbi getting married on a black sand beach in Hawaii. She wanted them to adopt and raise children together. She just wanted to live a happy life with her better half. Emani knew that if only she could tell her sisters about her and Bobbi, they wouldn't have to continue hiding their love for each other. They could finally bring their relationship out of the closet.

Emani continued to stand in a daze not hearing a word Diamond said.

"Emani…you aight?" "Uhh, o'yeah…I'm cool. Who's shot is it?" Emani asked, snapping out of her trance.

"It's been your shot for the past ten minutes," Diamond said, exaggerating the time that past.

"Oh, you got jokes? Ok then, I don't see why you in a rush

for me to knock these balls down. But I'm a show you why I've always been the best in pool. Three in the left corner…four in the right side pocket…eight ball off the rail, in the left corner pocket…game!" Emani yelled.

"Looks like I gotta pay for lunch huh?" Diamond said, laying her pool stick down in defeat.

"You know it. I'm hungry too. Let's go over here, so I can see what you're buying me." Emani said.

They walked towards the restaurant area. The waiter sat them down and handed Emani and Diamond their menus.

"I think I want me some buffalo wings," Emani said, looking at her menu.

"Damn…he got a nice butt, don't he?" Diamond asked Emani, as the waiter walked away from their table.

"Yeah, it was nice," Emani said, not really interested.

"So what's going on with you? All day it seemed like you've been some where else." Diamond said.

"I'm all right. I just got a lot of stress on me. With this big case I got coming up. You know I'm representing Sammy "Chicken Neck" Merlino," Emani said with pride in her voice.

"Damn I forgot. Stori told me you was representing the Philadelphia mob boss," Diamond said smiling.

"Allegedly," Emani corrected Diamond.

"Allegedly my ass. You know he a mob boss and my big sister is gonna be the first black woman to represent the mob. You bad girl." Diamond said with excitement.

"Well, what can I say? The Cooper girls got it going on." Emani said.

"Sho' nuff…but seriously, you can't be letting your job stress you out. You gonna get old before your time. Now what you need is a man that knows how to lay dat pipe. So he can knock some of that stress out your ass. Now look over there. That guy in the black is a perfect candidate for you. Matter fact, I'll be right back."

Diamond got up and left before Emani could stop her. It didn't take Diamond no more than a minute to come back with the two guys that were sitting four tables down from them. Emani noticed the two guys had to be at least 6 foot 8 inches tall. She didn't want to be bothered, but Emani figured it wouldn't hurt to entertain the guy on behalf of her sister.

"May I join you?" One of the tall guys asked Emani, trying to come across smooth.

"It's a free country, do you." Emani said flatly.

Diamond and the two guys sat down.

"This my sister Emani, Emani this is Manuel and Clarence. They play basketball for the 76ers." Diamond said.

"Yeah? I got season tickets, so I go to the games all the time. It's funny though cause I can't recall ever seeing ya'll play." Emani said, making Mannuel and Clarence feel awkward.

"Well you know, this our first year." Clarence said, trying to save face.

"Rookies, huh? Well if you ever need a good lawyer give me a call." Emani said smiling at Clarence. She handed him her card...

"Aunt Bobbi, can we play the video games before we eat?" Bobbi's niece Kayla asked as they walked up the steps of Dave and Buster's. "My favorite niece can do whatever she wants to do," Bobbi said.

Bobbi and Kayla entered Dave and Buster's. They walked towards the back where all the video games were located. As Bobbi walked past the restaurant area she noticed Emani sitting at a table smiling in a guy's face and handing him her number.

"I don't believe this shit. I'm fuckin' stressin, can't eat because of this bitch, and she out here fuckin with a guy of all people. Well fuck this we're through for real now." Bobbi thought. "This bitch gonna disrespect me like this. Fuck that, she gonna get hers."

Bobbi and Kayla walked past Emani just as Emani handed her business card to Clarence. Emani noticed Bobbi out the corner of her eye. Judging Bobbi's facial expression, Emani knew Bobbi had seen her. Emani's heart told her to drop everything she was doing and chase after Bobbi. Emani stayed where she was because of the fear of having her sister look down upon her and having her lifestyle exposed.

"Best believe, as soon as I get a chance, I'm going to see my baby Bobbi." Emani thought, hoping that she wasn't too late to get Bobbi back.

CHAPTER 13

"I don't believe it's raining all hard like this and I just got my hair done. I'm ready to postpone this date." Stori thought while getting dressed.

Ring...ring...ring.

"Hello," Stori answered.

"Girl, you ain't leave yet?" Tori asked.

"It's all raining out there. I'm ready to call him up and tell him I'm not going."

"No you not gonna do that. You acting like you going on this date to have a good time or something. You know this is strictly business. You suppose to get in good with him so we can set this lame up. I know I can make this my last job, feel me?"

"You right, even though I just got my hair tossed up and it's looking fierce. Messing it up in the rain will be worth it. After I set up my master plan."

"Well look, I'm not gonna hold you up. Be careful though and handle your business."

"You know I will. I'll call you when I get back."

As soon as Stori hung up her house phone her cell phone started ringing.

"Hello, may I speak to Stori?" Skeam asked.

"This is she."

"So what's up? Are we still on or what?"

"Yeah, we still on. I was just ready to call you." Stori said, looking in the mirror.

"You sure you don't want me to pick you up? Being as though it's raining and everything."

"Naw, let's just meet at 30th Street Station." Stori never let anybody know where she lives, except family.

"Ok. I'll be there in a half hour."

"I'll see you in a half hour then," Stori said hanging up the phone.

Stori walked into 30th Street Station an hour after she hung the phone up with Skeam. She wore a Roberto Cavalli pants set with a pair of Manolo Blahnik stilletos. Stori knew she was looking good. Skeam spotted Stori as soon as she walked through the doors.

"Damn, she's beautiful," Skeam thought. From the first time Skeam met Stori he thought she was special. He couldn't wait for this first date, because he'd been thinking about Stori day and night. Skeam knew he had to do something special for this woman.

"Hey you!" Skeam said approaching Stori.

"Hi," Stori said, shaking out her Chanel umbrella.

"Is the rain slowing up out there?"

"Hell no. I almost melted out there." Stori said, wiping off her clothes.

"As sweet as you look, you might be right," Skeam said, looking Stori up and down.

"I was ready to postpone this. I hate the rain." Stori said, as she checked her clothes making sure that mud hadn't splattered on them.

"I'm glad you didn't cancel because I would have been heartbroken. But hold up one second. I'm a see if I can play weatherman." Skeam said.

He pulled out his cell phone and dialed a number. Stori looked at Skeam wondering what he was talking about.

"I just got off the phone wit my peeps and they told me it's not raining in Cali," Skeam said, with a serious face.

"What does that have to do with us? We in Philly." Stori said, with her hands on her hips.

"We ain't got to be. I can make a call right now to get my jet fueled up. We can be over in Cali in no time." Skeam said, flipping his phone back open.

"Is you serious because I don't even know you like that."

"Come on now, I'm harmless. All I want to do is make it my purpose to make this the best day you ever had in your life. So if I have to change the weather for you to make that happen, so be it."

"I…I'm not even dressed for California," Stori said, looking down at her clothes.

"You don't have to worry about that. Just tell me you'll go and we can go shopping when we get down there." Skeam said, making his face resemble the face of a sad puppy.

Stori looked at Skeam for a minute. "Damn, he's fine as shit", Stori thought. Skeam wore a pair of Marithe Francois Girbaud jeans with the shirt to match. He had on an Avirex jacket and a pair of black Chukka boots. Stori couldn't believe how sharp Skeam's hair cut and beard were shaped up. She just loved how he wore his hair in a ceasar, dark all the way around. His waves were real thick as his hair had a pattern of a beehive.

"Let me stop lustin over this boy. I suppose to be here on business", Stori thought, wanting to stay focused.

"Please," Skeam said, folding his hands as if he were praying.

"Aight, I'll go. You better show me a good time though." Stori said teasing Skeam.

"I'll try my best, but right now let's get to the airport."

"What about my car?" "You can leave it here and get in the car with me."

"Let's be out then," Stori said.

Skeam led the way outside to his Ferrari 360 spider.

"Oh, this is cute," Stori said, looking at Skeam's car.

"Cute? A puppy is cute. This car right here is a beast." Skeam replied, opening the door for Stori.

"I'm sorry, did I hit a sore spot?"

"Naw I'm straight. If it wasn't raining like it was and I thought you could handle it. I would let you drive." Skeam said, placing the key in the ignition.

"Hold up...what you tryin to say, I can't drive or something?" Stori said, slightly offended.

"I'm sorry. Did I hit a sore spot?" Skeam asked smiling.

"Ok I had that coming to me." Stori said. She admired how Skeam flipped it right back on her.

Skeam turned the key in the ignition and "Prince's" song *Adore* came through the Bose speakers crystal clear.

"Boy, what you know about Prince?" Stori asked, surprised that Skeam played Prince, her favorite artist. Stori was expecting some Biggie or Tupac, or any kind of rap music, but not Prince.

"What I know about the artist formally known as Prince? Hold up, let me give you a little taste of my skills." Skeam said clearing his throat. "If one day God struck me blind, your beauty I'd still see/ love's too weak to define, just what you mean to me".

Skeam sang along to Prince's song *Adore*, all off key.

"Please, can you stop? You're killing my favorite song." Stori said laughing at how horrible he sounded singing.

"Fine, I guess you don't know talent when you see it." Skeam said.

"God gave you a gift to rap. Singing is not your forte', sorry." Stori said, patting Skeam on his shoulder.

"Aight watch, my next album I bring out. I'm a sing on the whole album." Skeam said as he pulled out into traffic.

"Please don't do that, cause if you do, instead of going double platinum, you'll be going double rusty."

"Oh...you got the full package, huh? You're beautiful and funny."

"Well you know...call it like you see it."

Stori and Skeam talked and laughed like they knew each other for years. Before they knew it, they were at the airport.

"I thought we were going to the Philadelphia airport?" Stori asked looking around.

"Naw, this ain't that type of airport. They just have private airstrips here. See, that's my jet right there, the silver one." Skeam said, pointing at his jet. It was fueled and ready for takeoff.

"You said that like you're talking about a car or something," Stori said, still staring at the jet.

"It's not like that. I'm very humble and thankful for everything I got. I just don't let any of it go to my head." Skeam said, driving towards his jet.

"I can respect that. Now do you have some Moet or Crissy on board?" Stori asked, becoming more comfortable with Skeam.

"I think I can pull that off for you." Skeam answered with a smile.

"How are you today, Mr. Skeam?" The pilot asked as Skeam and Stori boarded the jet.

"I'm good Jeffrey." Skeam said, shaking the pilot's hand.

"Hello maam, please...watch your step," Jeffrey said to Stori, extending his hand to escort her onto the plane.

"Hi," Stori said, as she looked around the interior of the jet.

"Do you like it?" Skeam asked. He noticed Stori's mouth open as she looked around. This is nicer than my living room at home. I love it."

"I'm glad you like it. Make yourself comfortable. My jet is your jet," Skeam said.

He felt tempted to hold Stori in his arms. Stori sat down on the plush leather chair next to the window. She couldn't help but to feel like a kid ready to celebrate her first birthday party. She struggled to maintain her composure.

"Let me get you that glass of Crissy you asked about," Skeam said, pulling out a bottle of Cristal that was already sitting in a bucket of ice. Skeam took a seat right across from Stori after pouring them both a glass of champagne.

"So, is this how you treat all your women?" Stori asked Skeam. She sat back in the plush leather seat and crossed her shapely legs.

"Believe it or not, you are the first woman besides my momma to ride in my jet," Skeam said sipping his Cristal.

"You said believe it or not, so I'm a say, not" Stori said.

"Stori, I wouldn't lie to you. I haven't been in a serious relationship for the past five years and five years ago when I was committed to someone I didn't have my own jet," Skeam said with an honest look on his face.

"What makes me so special?"

"I don't know, but I'm hoping I can find out."

Skeam looked deep into Stori's eyes. Stori tried to hide the fact that she was blushing as she looked at the clouds outside her window.

"Would you like a refill?" Skeam asked, looking at Stori's empty glass.

"Yes please," Stori said holding out her champagne glass. Skeam got up to refill Stori's glass as Stori kept her eyes on him.

"Damn, he smells so good and why is +he always saying the right things," Stori thought as she inhaled Skeam's scent.

Stori found it hard not to get comfortable with Skeam. Although Stori liked Skeam's style, she knew she couldn't mix business with pleasure.

"I'm here to set this nigga up and that's it," Stori said to herself over and over again, reminding herself that this wasn't a real date.

Before they finished the bottle of Cristal the plane landed in sunny California. Stori couldn't do anything but smile when she got off the plane. She enjoyed the air at eighty-five degrees without humidity. The warm sunny day made her body feel good.

"Are you glad we came?"

"Yeah...this is cool, but it would be even better if we did that shopping thing you was talking about." Stori said, putting on her best baby face.

"Say no more," Skeam said as he led Stori to his awaiting Lamborghini.

"Now this is a beast, a beautiful beast," Stori said.

"I'm glad you like it," Skeam said.

He opened the suicide doors for Stori. Once Skeam got in the car he turned on the car and searched for a CD to play. He pushed the play button on the remote control and Jodeci's *Forever My Lady* came through the speakers. Right away, Skeam started singing again. "So you're having my baby/ and it means so much to me/ there's nothing more precious/ than to raise a family."

"Noooooooo, please stop before my ears start bleeding," Stori begged, covering her ears with her hands. She and Skeam started laughing until tears came to their eyes.

Skeam drove to Rodeo Drive to visit all the designer shops such as Gucci, Fendi, Chanel, and a host of other high priced clothing boutiques. Stori had more bags than she could carry as she skipped from shop to shop. Stori shopped until her feet hurt so much that she couldn't shop any further. She never thought that was possible.

"Let's go somewhere and relax," Stori said.

"Are you sure, cause we still haven't hit all the shops yet. Plus you didn't even put a dent in my platinum card. That jawn got a few more thousand swipes on it," Skeam said full of energy.

"I never thought I would ever say this in my life, but I'm tired of shopping." Stori said, as she stretched her back out.

"Are you hungry?" Skeam asked.

"I'm starving," Stori answered, rubbing her flat stomach.

"So what do you have a taste for?" Skeam asked, walking Stori toward the Lamborghini.

"You know, I've been down here three other times and always wanted to go to Roscoe's Chicken and Waffles, but something always came up, so I never got a chance to go." Stori said, as her mouth watered a little bit.

"That's what's up. Roscoe's is one of my favorite spots down here. I know you'll enjoy it."

On the way to Roscoe's Stori kept looking back at the van that followed them.

"Relax Stori, your clothes and stuff are safe," Skeam said, looking over at Stori.

"I know, it's just that I still can't believe you had to call your people's up, so they could bring a van down for all the stuff you bought me,"

"Well all them bags wasn't fitting in here. We barely got all those bags in the van." Skeam said with a smile.

"I know I did get a lot of stuff. Thank you Skeam."

"Your welcome Stori."

They arrived at Roscoe's where they ate, drank, and talked for hours. Everything seemed strange to Stori because she never opened up to a man before. She never gave them a chance to really get to know her. Now Stori found herself opening up more to Skeam. To her surprise she was enjoying every minute she spent with him.

"So, all this time we spent together and I don't know your real name yet." Stori said as she sipped on her iced tea.

"That's a sensitive subject right there."

"What you mean by that?"

"I'm saying, I don't like it."

"Your name can't be that bad."

"I'm not telling you," Skeam said, sitting back in his chair.

"What if I give you a kiss," Stori said, not believing she said that because she never kissed on the first date.

"Damn, how can I refuse that deal. I've been mesmerized by your juicy lips all day," Skeam said making Stori blush.

"Well, what is it?" Stori asked again, thinking Skeam's name couldn't be that bad.

"Where's my kiss?"

"Here it go. "Stori said.

She walked around the table to Skeam. She sat in the seat next to him and placed her hand on Skeam's thigh. Skeam gently placed both his hands on the back of Stori's neck and slowly guided her lips to his. They both licked their lips before they kissed making sure they were as moist as possible. When they started kissing Stori felt that it was the most sensual kiss she ever had. Neither of them used their tongues to explore each other's mouth. There just was something about the kiss that made both of them feel warm inside.

"That was nice," Stori said as she broke away from the kiss before things got too heated.

"I know and I never kiss on the first date," Skeam said, licking his full pink lips savoring the taste of Stori's lips.

"Me neither, so consider yourself special. Now let's get down to business. Tell me this horrible name of yours." Stori said, rubbing her hands together.

"Aight I'll tell you, but promise me you won't laugh."

"Cross my heart, hope to die, stick a needle in my eye."

"Aight, remember you said that."

"I will."

"My name is Oscar...Oscar Cecil Smalls the Third."

"Tell me you lying," Stori said as she tried her best to hold in her laugh, but was quickly losing the battle.

"See, you promised me you wouldn't laugh. I knew I shouldn't have told you." Skeam said, crossing his arms and sucking his teeth like a big kid.

"I'm sorry for laughing but you don't look like no Oscar Cecil Smalls the Third," Stori said, holding in her smile.

"See, I never tell nobody my name," Skeam said, slouching further down in his seat.

"Here, let me make it up to you." Stori said, as she sat on Skeam's lap and gave him another kiss. "Damn, I could get used to this." Skeam thought.

Stori just smiled and kissed Skeam again. As Stori sat on Skeam's lap, she could feel his manhood stiffen under her. Stori closed her eyes and finally slid her tongue inside of Skeam's mouth. She slightly moved her butt up and down Skeam's erection that was threatening to pop out of his jeans. Stori opened her eyes and saw a little Mexican kid staring at her. Stori quickly stopped kissing Skeam, jumped off of his lap, and sat in her own chair.

"What's wrong?" Skeam asked, wanting to continue the kiss.

"Look around, I think we forgot where we were at," Stori said, with her head down and feeling a little embarrassed. Skeam looked around and saw everybody staring at them.

"Yeah, I think we got caught up in the moment."

"You ready to go?" Stori asked.

"Yeah, I know a spot a little more intimate," Skeam said, rubbing his hands together.

"Well let's go then," Stori said, totally forgetting about setting up a plan to rob Skeam.

CHAPTER 14

Flea called a meeting for him and his squad of young thugs. Flea had been recruiting more young guys than Uncle Sam. He only wanted the hungriest and most dedicated young thugs on his team. Just like he used all white women for his credit card scam, he needed hungry young thugs for his other scams. There wasn't a con out there that Flea hadn't mastered. If there was some money out there ready for taking, Flea and his squad were going to be the ones to take it.

Flea had recently received a stack of certified checks that he needed to move. His team of young thugs were going to move the checks for him. Once all nine of his young "buls" arrived at the meeting spot, Flea got down to business.

"A Tek, why is you late coming to my meeting?" Flea asked the last young "bul" that got to the meeting.

"You said 6 o'clock right?" Tek asked Flea as he looked at his watch.

"Yeah, I said 6 o'clock. It's 6:07. If I told ya'll once, I'll tell ya'll twice. Time is money, so be on time." "My fault ol' head," Tek said as he took a seat.

"Ya'll ready to get this paper?" Flea asked, wanting to build the group's excitement.

"Ol head, you know how we get down. If it's money out there to be made, we gonna make it." Murk said, speaking for him and the rest of the eight money hungry young thugs.

"See, that's the motivation I want out of ya'll. This paper

is plentiful and we all can eat. We just got to get it." Flea said, limping back and forth.

His young "buls" sat there hanging onto every word he said.

"So how are we gonna get at this paper?" Murk asked.

"I'm ready to school ya'll now on that, so listen up." Flea said.

Flea proceeded to lay his plan out to his young thugs. Flea first told them about the certified checks. He explained to them how he came across a stash of authentic certified checks, and that all they had to do was move the checks. Flea told them that buying stuff from out the newspaper was the way to move the checks. They were to look through the classifieds, and see who was selling what. Once they identified something they liked, they would call the seller to set up a time to see the merchandise. After meeting the seller, they would look over the merchandise, and then tell the seller they wanted the merchandise for the agreed upon price. Then they ask the unsuspected victim would it be ok to pay with a certified check. Nine times out of ten, the victim would be more than happy to accept the certified checks. As far as the victims were concerned, the checks were guaranteed by the bank. Flea also told his young protéges to let the victims know that they could only bring by the certified check on Friday after work. That way when they meet the victim between 6 and 6:30 p.m., all the banks would be closed. Then they would be home free.

After Flea made fake driver's licenses for everybody, he sent his young "buls" out to handle their business. If the con goes as planned, the young "buls" would have everything from computers and jewelry to motorcycles and pit bull puppies. Anything that the young "buls" could get a hold of, they would flip it into a profit somehow.

"Murk, let me holla at you for a minute," Flea asked.

"What up ol' head?"

"Look, I need you to gather up some of your homie's so I can get this instant credit thing jumpin."

"No problem."

"Now I don't need none of your homie's that be smokin blunts all day. This instant credit hustle requires you to remember a lot of information. So I need somebody on point. I'm coming to you with this because I see your earning potential, plus I know I can trust you. I know you're ready to get paid, am I right?"

"Put it like this…a sucka is being born every minute and I'm a take full advantage of that." Murk answered.

"I like how you put that. I'm a put you under my wing and show you how to really get this money. I can't do this shit forever. I'm a have to retire soon, and when I do, I'm a give you all the knowledge you need to keep this empire flowing. All you gotta do is kick me back a couple dollars a week and the rest will be yours."

Flea pulled out a Black and Mild cigar and lit it. Flea had been keeping his eye on Murk for quite some time now. He knew his team of young "buls" were all hungry and ready to eat. There was something about Murk that made him stand out more than the others. As Murk was the perfect candidate for taking over his business, Flea knew he would have to teach him a few more ends and outs. Flea thought that when he stepped down, the business could reach its greatest potential with Murk as the head.

"Yo, that's what's up Flea. I'm tellin' you, I might be a conniving, deceitful, and a low down grimmey nigga, but I'm loyal to those that are loyal to me. So if you do decide to give me that chance, I'm a prove to you that you made the right decision."

"Well you already a step ahead in the game, cause being conniving and deceitful is a major part in this con game. I also pride myself on being a good judge of character and when I see you, I see me 25 years ago. So I know you won't disappoint me." Flea said, as he blew smoke out his mouth.

"I got you, but if we're done, I'm a go and start handling this business. We got vics to take down." Murk said, extending his hand out so he could give Flea a handshake.

"OK, young buc, go handle your business. We'll talk later on that."

Murk turned around on his heels to leave the meeting spot.

"If that young bul stay on his job, he could go a long way," Flea thought as he plucked ashes from his Black and Mild.

Riing…riing..riiiing…

"Hello," Flea said answering his cell phone.

"Hey babe, it's me. Like, Suzy got herself in a jam and got locked up down the 35th." Becky said, in her white girl voice.

"Locked up for what?" Flea asked as he was already leaving the meeting spot heading to his car.

"Evidently the salesman remembered Suzy from a couple of months ago, when she hit their store under the name Marie Osufchuck." Becky said, knowing Flea would take care of everything. "So when she went back to the same store using the name Lori Riley, the salesman got suspicious and called the police."

"Didn't I tell ya'll a thousand times not to hit the same store twice. Especially if the same salesperson is in there," Flea said agitated.

"I know honey, I don't know what she was thinking about."

"You don't know what she was thinking bout? Ya'll gonna know when I start crackin heads around this bitch."

The thing he hated the most was stupidity. Becky sat quiet on the other end of the phone. She knew from experience not to say anything when Flea was mad like this.

"Aight look, if you hear from her again, tell her to hold tight and I'll be right down to bail her out, hear me?"

"I hear you, but I already told her that. I also told her to keep her mouth shut until you get there."

"Good job baby, I know I can always count on you."

Flea hung up his phone and climbed into his car. "Damn, everything that glitters ain't always gold. Everything was going so smooth lately. I guess it's true what they say, 'Laugh now, cry later'," Flea thought, as he drove to Broad Street and Champlost Avenue to pick up Suzy at the 35th police district.

CHAPTER 15

The "Playground" on Hunting Park and Germantown Avenue was jammed packed with go-go dancers, and drug dealers who were ready to spend their crack sale earnings. This was a special night because the strippers from New York were coming down to battle the strippers from Philly. The event was advertised for weeks. Everybody in the club was anxious to see a good show. What most of the people didn't know was that the battle was a gimmick to get more money into the club. That didn't matter as long as the ballers saw titties and asses. All the top notch dancers in the city were there. Lyin' Leon was the MC for the night. They called him Lyin Leon because every time he ended a sentence, he always said "I ain't ly'in!" Everybody in the club knew this would be a night to remember. All the ballers poured in the front door of the club.

"If a bitch can't make no money tonight, she needs to fall back and get out the game." Alize said to Diamond as she looked around at all the money makers throughout the smoke filled club.

"I know a few of these niggas is gonna pay all my bills this month," Diamond said, talking over Maxwell's song *Fortunate* that the DJ had blaring through the speakers.

"Girl, this is definitely gonna be a good night," Alize said as she checked out her outfit.

"These New York chicks are in here thick," Diamond said, looking around at all the new faces.

"Don't none of them look as good as us. So they not gonna

stop any of our cash flow." Alize said, knowing that by the end of the night her pockets would still be fat.

"Oh, I'm not even worried about that. I'm just trippin on how they talk. You hear their accents,it's crazy ain't it?" Diamond asked Alize.

"Yeah, their accents are real thick. They must be deep in the hood of New York." Alize said.

"I like how they talk. Like the one girl…you know the Puerto Rican girl that be dancing in the beginning of Spike Lee's movie *Do The Right Thing*, Diamond said.

"Oh, you talkin bout Rosie Perez."

"Yeah, yeah…that's her. Now her accent has to be the thickest New York accent in the entire Big Apple."

"Yeah her accent is thick as shit. But like I said earlier, ain't none of these New York chicks a threat to me. So I'm not worried about them." Alize said with her Philly swagger.

"Speaking of a threat, have you seen dat crazy bitch Precious?" Diamond asked Alize.

"Naw, I haven't seen her since we beat dat bitch down and I pissed on her," Alize said smiling.

"Well keep an eye out for that bitch. I know she's not gonna let that shit ride. She's gonna want some revenge. You know she don't got it all." Diamond said, knowing that no one should ever be underestimated.

"Fuck her, I'm not worrying about that bitch. Shit, she can get it again if she want it." Alize said, not wanting to hear Diamond's logic.

"Look girl, just keep your eyes open that's all." Diamond said upset that Alize' wasn't taking the situation serious.

"Whatever." Alize said, as she looked around the club trying to figure out which baller had the most paper.

"Aight then, let's just go and get this money," Diamond said, not wanting to draw out the conversation.

"That's the best thing you said all night," Alize said as guys pulled on her arm as she mingled through the crowd.

Champagne bottles popped, blunts sparked, and everybody stood around having a good time. Three hours later, Diamond and Alize had over $2,000 a piece.

"Damn these niggas are generous as shit tonight," Alize' said, as she counted her bundle of currency.

"Yeah...I know, but I'm tired and hot as shit. I'm ready to get out of this sweat shop." Diamond said, wiping sweat from off her forehead.

"Girl, are you crazy? These niggas pockets ain't empty yet. I wanna bleed these wanna be hustlas dry." Alize' said not wanting to miss out on all the genoristy that was going around the club that night.

"We made enough money tonight, let's be out."

"Is you crazy? You acting as if these niggas be handing out their money like this all the time. These niggas wanna be happy-go-lucky giving out their change. I'm a be happy-go-lucky right with them while I'm stuffin my bag with all them dead presidents." Alize' said, giving Diamond a crazy look that said "you stupid for wanting to leave."

"I feel you, but I'm tired as shit. We don't have to get every last dime in here. We got 'em for a nice piece of change tonight. Let's just be out,and be thankful for what we already got."

"Naw, fuck dat...you can bounce if you want, but I'm not goin nowhere. If you do leave though, you crazy." Alize' said really wanting Diamond to stay.

"Well call mc crazy...but I'm leaving, I'm tired. Is you going to be ok?" Diamond asked, not wanting to leave Alize' by herself.

"Can I get a dance?" A guy asked Alize as he sipped on a glass of Remy Martin.

"Yeah...I'm a be aight," Alize said, as she walked away to give her customer a lap dance.

"I'll call you tomorrow." Diamond said, yelling at Alize's

back.

Diamond didn't know if Alize' heard her because Alize' never turned back around.

"Oh well, you can't please everybody," Diamond thought as she went to the dressing room to get changed.

"That shit was jumpin in there," Diamond thought as she started her Benz and pulled off.

Back in the club, Alize' couldn't believe she made $4,867.

"I tried to tell Diamond's dumb ass to stay. But nooo, she was tired. Well fuck it, that's her loss." Alize' thought.

Alize' couldn't wait until she talked to Diamond tomorrow. She wanted to rub how much money she made in Diamond's face. The night was winding down and all the ballers were trying to get somebody to go to the motel with them.

"Let me get out of here now before these fools start acting crazy," Alize' thought, as she headed to the dressing room.

After getting dressed and turning down a bunch of guys trying to proposition her, Alize' finally made it outside. She parked around the corner, because the club was so full that night.

"Let me hurry up, and get out of here before another one of these guys says some foul shit out they mouth to me." Alize' thought, as she headed towards her truck. She took her keys out her pocket and disarmed her alarm. When Alize' reached for the door handle, she noticed a figure coming up on her side. It was too late to react as the aluminum bat came crashing down on her shoulder blade. Before Alize' could let out a scream, a wooden bat slammed into her mouth.

"Remember me...Remember me...Remember me!!!!" Precious said, swinging her wooden bat like a mad woman.

The wooden bat continued to strike Alize's defenseless body as Alize's body crumpled to the ground. Alize' wanted to scream badly, but couldn't because her mouth was filled with blood. Alize's scream attempts made a gurgling sound as the bats connected with every inch of her body.

"Precious watch out," Precious'cousin Shamia said, as she swung the aluminum bat, breaking Alize's knee cap.

"Yeah bitch, where your nut ass girl friend at? Believe me, she gonna get it too." Precious said to Alize'.

Precious' other cousin Aleen stood watch at the corner while Precious and Shamia tired themselves from pummeling Alize's motionless body.

"Hurry up ya'll, they starting to come out the club," Aleen said to Precious and Shamia.

"Come on, let's strip this bitch," Precious said, as she started ripping Alize's clothes off.

Shamia dug in Alize's bag and pulled out the $4,867 Alize'made that night.

"Damn, this bitch was shaking her ass hard tonight," Shamia said, flipping through the money.

"Grab the whole bag and let's be out," Precious said to Shamia.

Shamia grabbed everything and took it to their car which was sitting in front of Alize's truck. Once Shamia got in the car, she quickly looked over her shoulder. She made sure Precious and Aleen weren't coming. She quickly stuffed $600 in her bra.

"They'll never know," Shamia thought.

"Aleen...let's roll!" Precious yelled out as Aleen started jogging back towards her.

"Oh...I almost forgot, you still got that right?" Precious asked Aleen. "Yeah, it's right here," Aleen said, handing Precious a brown paper bag. Precious stood over Alize' and opened up the brown paper bag. Precious bended over to open Alize's mouth where she poured in the dog feces from the brown paper bag.

"You fuckin' pissed on me? Yeah, pay backs a bitch." Precious said.

She and Aleen jumped in their car. Shamia quickly pulled off leaving Alize' laying on the sidewalk wearing nothing but a pair of thongs with a toothless mouth full of shit.

Diamond pulled up to her house and started to feel bad for

leaving Alize by herself. They had a rule that they would always watch each other's back and never leave each other. "We made all this money. She just being greedy. She didn't even want to compromise with me. Fuck it…if she's mad at me, she'll forgive me sooner or later." Diamond justified to herself as she hit the remote to the garage door.

The garage door opened and Diamond pulled her Benz inside. She hit the remote again to let the garage door down. A dark figure dressed in all black slid under the garage door just before it shut. Little did Diamond know, the figure dressed in black was ready to give her a rude awakening.

CHAPTER 16

"So what da fuck is up with your sister?" Zikeema asked Tori, referring to Stori.

"I don't know. She don't ever take this long to plan a job. This set up has been going on for over a month. She know I need this last job, so I can fall back and retire." Tori said.

She and Zikeema sat in Zikeema's Range Rover eating fish fried rice and drinking Akbar juice from the Garden of Bilal's restaurant on Stenton Avenue.

"I know her stinking ass barely returns my phone calls. I don't know what's goin on with her, but push come to shove, I'll set Skeam up myself. I already know where he live at." Zikeema said.

"You're right, Stori has been on some other shit lately. Let's give her a little while longer though. You gotta think, if she's taking this long, she must be trying to hit da "bul" for every dime he got." Tori said, convinced that Stori was masterminding the perfect job.

"You probably right, but if she take too long, I'm doin this without her." Zikeema said.

"Aight, we can do that. Right now though, I need you to take me home. I know my husband is missin seeing my gorgeous face around the house." Tori said, as she checked the time on her Cartier watch.

"Bitch, you ain't that cute." Zikeema said playfully.

Zikeema started her Range Rover and pulled off. Zikeema

was tired of waiting on Stori to call all the shots. Every job they did together, they all had to wait on Stori. Zikeema knew she could plan a robbery by herself and now she was ready to prove it.

"Girl, give me a call tomorrow," Tori said as she got out of Zikeema's truck.

"Yeah…yeah, I'll call you. Just take your hot ass in the house. I know Jerome is gonna knock the bottom out of your draws tonight." Zikeema said, as she turned down the music in her truck.

"You know it." Tori said.

Tori ran in the house. Zikeema pulled off laughing knowing that her sister had a wonderful marriage.

"I need to settle down and get married, maybe have a couple kids...naw, I got too much to do. I don't need nothing or nobody slowing me down. Maybe I'll get married later on in life. Right now the streets is calling." Zikeema thought.

Zikeema drove around aimlessly, not wanting to go home. She went to all the hot spots in North Philly, but wasn't nothing jumping. After leaving the Eagle Bar at Broad Street and Erie Avenue, Zikeema decided to head toward West Philly. "Yeah, I'm a shoot down West and see what them niggas doing down "Conversations"", Zikeema thought, feeling restless.

Riing…riing…riiing.

Zikeema reached for her cell phone that laid on the passenger's seat.

"Hello," Zikeema said, turning down her Mary J. Blige, *My Life* CD.

"Yo…we need to talk," Ishmael said flatly.

"Damn, no Hi Zikeema, a what's goin on, or something?"

"I would of if you deserved it."

"Ok, enough with the games. If you got something to say, spit it out." Zikeema said becoming a little ticked off with Ishamael's attitude.

"I wanna know about us. Where do I stand at in your life?"

"What you mean, where you stand at? You are my man, my love."

"Why don't I feel like I'm your man, or your love?"

"Ishmael, I don't know why. You have to tell me why you feel that way."

"Zikeema, we never spend no time together and when we do get to spend some time together, you quick to get up and leave. I swear I'm getting tired of this. Now I don't want to give you no ultimatum or anything, but if we are going to continue this relationship, things are going to have to change."

"Ishmael you're absolutely right. Why don't I come over there right now so we can talk and work this thing out."

Zikeema realized that when it came to Ishmael she knew that she had a good man that she definitely didn't want lose.

"I'm not home right now."

"Where you at stinky butt?" Zikeema said, ready to make love to her man so she could ease his mind.

"I'm up Atlantic City with Money Grip," Ishamael said, talking about his cousin.

"Stinky Butt, I wanted to go to Atlantic City," Zikeema pouted.

"I'm sorry baby. Money grip called me at the last minute and dragged me out the house. It was a spur of the moment thing."

"You could've called me." Zikeema said, thinking about how casinos are filled with excitement.

"Baby I'll just get with you when I get back, ok?" "Fine then." Zikeema said still pouting.

"Baby are you ok?" "Yeah, I'm ok"

"Well say you love me then."

"I miss you Stinky Butt and I love you,"

"See that's how I like hearing my baby talk. Now I'll come through when I get back down Philly ok?"

"OK baby and bring me back some of that money you're

going to win."

"You know I will…aight here I come. Baby I'm a go. Money Grip is calling me. He's trying to get over at them Black Jack tables."

"Don't let me hold you up. I love you and have a good time."

"I love you too. I'll see you later."

"Fuck it, he's not going to be the only one winning some money," Zikeema said to herself, as she turned up Mary J. Blige's song *You Got To Believe*. Conversations was a small bar in West Philly, right off of Haverford Avenue. The bar area was downstairs. Upstairs was where all the hustlers were shooting dice. Zikeema parked her truck on Haverford Ave and walked around the corner to "Conversations". When Zikeema walked in, she had to adjust her eyes to the dark smoke filled room. Downstairs was packed as people drank and talked over the loud juke box which was playing an old Keith Sweat song.

"Can I buy you a drink, ma?" A guy asked Zikeema when she walked up to the bar.

"No thank you sweety, but let me buy you a drink. Bartender, what is this handsome man drinking?"

"He's drinking Hennessy straight up," the barmaid said as she stood there wiping out a glass with her towel.

"Well give him a double shot of Hennessy and give me a thug passion. I want the orange Alize with dat," Zikeema said, pulling a $50 bill out her Dolce and Gabbana handbag.

"Damn ma, I ain't used to this. Most women expect you to buy them a drink. Not the other way around."

"Well I'm not like most women," Zikeema said, waiting for her drink.

"You right about that. Why don't you sit next to me so we can get to know each other a little better." The guy said, patting the empty stool next to him.

"As tempting as that is, I'm a have to say no. I mean, I don't think my boyfriend would like that." Zikeema said, handing the barmaid the $50 to pay for the drink.

"I can respect that, but if dude fucks up I'll be right here to capitalize on his mistake," the guy said, looking straight into Zikeema's eyes.

"I'm a remember that, but until then, enjoy your drink." Zikeema said, walking away.

"Miss…Miss…you forgot your change," the barmaid shouted.

"No I didn't. Keep it."

Zikeema headed upstairs. But before Zikeema reached the top of the steps, she heard all the gamblers betting on the dice game. She causally walked up wanting to see how much money was in the game. Zikeema stood to the side sipping on her thug passion. She was a little upset to see they weren't betting big. "Oh well, I'll take these broke niggas few hundred dollars," she thought.

"I'll bet you $50 you wrong on that six," Zikeema said to the shooter in the middle.

Like always, all the gamblers stopped to look at Zikeema. Not believing someone this fine and sophisticated would be wanting to shoot dice with them.

"Damn…you fine as shit, but that $50 you holdin is even finer, so that's a bet," the shooter said, shaking the dice.

After three rolls, the guy crapped out. Letting Zikeema get on the dice was a major mistake. She hit number after number, collecting the few dollars that was in the game.

"Damn, why can't my shot be on fire like this when big money is in the game?" Zikeema thought to herself, as she watched guy after guy, leave the game. Zikeema broke everybody in the game after forty-five minutes. She still wished the game was a high roller's game, but was still satisfied with her winnings. Walking away with $985, Zikeema figured she'd go spend her winnings at the King of Prussia mall tomorrow. Zikeema walked back downstairs to have one more drink before she went home for the night. When she got down there, she hoped the guy she bought the drink for earlier was still there. Not that she wanted to get with him or anything, even though she did think he was cute. Zikeema was too much in love with Ishmael. Zikeema felt that the guy was just easy to talk to and she wanted to kill some time. After looking up and down the bar for him, Zikeema realized he was gone.

"Oh well, forget the small talk. I'll just drink my drink and go home." Zikeema thought as she pulled out a Black and Mild and lit it. A habit she picked up from her Uncle Flea. After turning down about ten different guys' advances, Zikeema finally finished her drink. Zikeema paid the barmaid and made her way to her Range Rover.

Everything was quiet when Zikeema got outside. The night was unusually warm for early March. Zikeema was still full of energy, but she figured she'd take it in for the night and watch a movie. When Zikeema grabbed the door handle to get in the truck, somebody came up from behind her and stuck a gun in her back.

"Damn…I'm slippin," Zikeema thought as her body froze. Zikeema knew she was about to get stuck up by one of the guys she just broke in the crap game.

"Look…the money is in my purse. Go ahead…take it all… take everything," Zikeema said not wanting to get shot over her chump change.

"What bitch? You robbed me for $190,000 and you talkin bout take the money out of your funky ass purse. I'm a take your money aight. That and your life you dumb bitch."

Zikeema's heart dropped knowing right away who it was. It was Big Tyme she robbed a few weeks ago with the money suit. Feeling death knocking at her door, Zikeema knew she had to think fast.

"Look, I don't know what your talking about," Zikeema said.

"Bitch keep playing dumb and I'm a put a slug in your spinal cord right now. It ain't no coincidence that I take over $67,000 from a girl and two hours later a girl in a mask robs me. You don't need a rocket scientist to figure out it was your stupid ass. I swear when I saw you coming out of Conversations, my dick got hard. I been looking for you for a minute now." Big Tyme said with a smile on his face.

"Please wait, let me explain," Zikeema said, stalling for time.

Zikeema desperately tried to figure out a way to get out of her sticky situation.

"You ain't explaining shit. We goin to your house to get my money. Then I might give you some dick before I kill your dead ass." Big Tyme said, grinding his teeth.

Zikeema knew her time on earth was up. She was determined not to let Big Tyme take both her life and her money. If she was going to die, the money she had in her safe would be left to her sisters.

"God, I know my life hasn't been right, but please take me with open arms." Zikeema said to herself before turning around to face the guy that was going to take her life.

"Bitch, did I say turn around?"

"Fuck you nigga, my pops and uncle ain't raise no soft bitches. They raised five soldiers. So that money I took from your nut ass, you might as well forget about it. Take it on the chin and charge it to da game," Zikeema said, as a tear escaped her left eye.

"Well take this on the chin," Big Tyme said with anger, as he cocked the hammer back.

He aimed his .357 magnum at Zikeema's face.

"You know I'm a strong believer in karma, so this will definitely come back on you," Zikeema said with a smile.

Tears continued to roll down her cheeks.

"Yeah, just like it's coming back on you now. So fuck all that bullshit you talkin, just get ready to meet your maker." Big Tyme said, gripping the gun tighter.

"Fuck you and go to Hell", Zikeema screamed out.

"No, you first."

Boom!

Blood, brains, and bones covered Zikeema's face and head. She was surprised she didn't feel any pain. She always wondered what death was like. Her sisters always told her she was obsessed with death. Zikeema always disagreed with that. She loved life to much to be obsessed with death. At times, it would cross her mind how she was going to die. But Zikeema felt that everybody thought about death at least once or twice in their life. Zikeema often wondered was her death going to be her ending or was it a new beginning for her in a new place. Zikeema was never big on religion. She always questioned if God did exist and how He could take her mother and father away from her. Now that death was knocking at her door, she found herself praying that there was a God, as she tried to reach out to Him. She hoped that she was on her way to Heaven and not Hell. Zikeema swore she could feel her body and soul floating away, as her entire life flashed in front of her. She wanted to see where she was going, so she tried to open her eyes. Something warm was on her face blocking her vision. "Please God, let me see again," Zikeema said once again praying to the same God she avoided her whole life. Zikeema wiped her eyes and tried to open them again. This time she was able to see and she was surprised of what she saw. Instead of the pearly gates, Zikeema saw Big Tyme laid out on the sidewalk with his head blown off. She looked up and saw the guy she bought the drink for earlier standing over top of the faceless body. Smoke was still rising from the guy's gun. He stood over Big Tyme's lifeless body holding a big gun in his hand.

"Shorty, you aight?" the guy asked, gently grabbing Zikeema by the shoulders.

"You...you saved my life," Zikeema said, finally realizing that she wasn't dead.

She attempted to wipe the blood, brains, and bone off of her.

"Look, we'll talk about that later. Right now we need to get outta here. Is this your whip?" The guy said surveying his surroundings and pointing to Zikeema's Range Rover.

"Yeah…yeah," Zikeema managed to get out of her mouth.

"Here give me your keys and get in."

Zikeema handed over her keys and got in the passenger side. The guy started the Range Rover and drove off.

"By the way, my name is Kyree," the guy said.

He took off his t-shirt and handed it to Zikeema so that she could wipe off Big Tyme's blood.

"Thank you," Zikeema said, taking the shirt from Kyree.

"So, do you have a name?"

"Oh…I'm sorry, my name is Zikeema."

"That's a pretty name for a pretty woman."

Zikeema sat there thinking, "How could this guy sit here and act like he didn't just shoot somebody's head off. Who does this guy think he is?"

Whoever he was, Zikeema knew she liked what she saw. After all, she owed him her life. She also knew she needed to reevaluate her relationship with God.

CHAPTER 17

"I can't believe this bitch is fuckin with my emotions like this. How can she be out on a date, with a fuckin man at that, of all fuckin people. Now she wanna blow my phone up like I'm going to answer it. I'm not being second to no one, especially no man." Bobbi thought as she wrecked her brain over Emani.

Ever since the day Bobbi saw Emani inside Dave and Buster's, she'd been unable to think straight. Bobbi found herself constantly calling out from work. She confined herself to her house drinking and smoking weed all day. Bobbi wasn't eating much. She noticed that she was losing a lot of weight. The worse Bobbi became, the more blame she put on Emani. Constantly she thought that Emani was at home having sex with the guy she saw her with at Dave and Buster's. Little did Bobbi know, Emani was home being more stressed out than she was.

Bobbi would never believe that, because the majority of the time she didn't know if she was coming or going. Bobbi decided to take a drive in her car. After a while she found herself parked in front of a restaurant on 10ᵗʰ and Oregon Avenue in South Philly. The restaurant was a mob hangout for Sammy "Chicken Neck" Merlino. Bobbi didn't know what she would say to the mob boss because she hadn't planned the trip down there. All she knew was she wanted to get back at Emani. After sitting in her car for a couple of hours, Bobbi finally got out and went inside the restaurant. All eyes were on her as she walked into the small restaurant. Bobbi quickly counted twelve Italian guys sitting around wearing tight sweat suits and an array of gold jewelry. She nervously looked around. Bobbi took in a deep breath. The smell of spaghetti and cigars invaded her nose. Always seeing Sammy "Chicken Neck" Merlino in the newspaper made it easy for Bobbi to spot him.

Just as Bobbi gathered the courage to walk over in Merlino's direction, a muscle bound goon stood in front of Bobbi blocking her path.

"Is there something I can help you wit over here?" The goon asked, as he stood there in his tight Fila sweat suit adjusting his crotch.

"Yes, I want to talk to Mr. Merlino." Bobbi uttered nervously.

"Mr. Merlino ain't seein nobody right now," the goon said, as he undressed Bobbi with his eyes.

"Well tell him this has to do with his lawyer, Miss Emani Cooper," Bobbi said, as she switched her 120 pounds from one leg to the other.

The goon looked Bobbi up and down before telling her to wait here. Bobbi started second guessing herself. Wondering what the hell she was doing there. She watched the goon walk over to his boss Merlino and whisper in his ear. Merlino bent over and looked at Bobbi.

Bobbi stood there scared out of her mind, ready to run as fast as she could out the front door. The goon walked back over to Bobbi. A large lump formed in her throat.

"Hold your arms out," the goon instructed Bobbi.

Bobbi reluctantly held out her arms. The goon began patting her body checking for weapons. Bobbi was visibly upset by the goon getting in his free feels.

"Joey…what are ya doin, huh? That's a lady." Merlino said, hollering at the goon.

"Mr. Merlino will see you now, follow me."

The goon lead Bobbi to the table where "Chicken Neck" Merlino was sitting.

"I'm sorry for my associate's rudeness. He's just a little over protective," Merlino said as he wiped spaghetti from his mouth with a napkin.

"That's ok, I understand," Bobbi said, as she stood there fidgety. "So how can I help you?" Merlino asked, impressed by Bobbi's beauty.

Bobbi looked down at the skinny Italian man who wore his jet black hair slicked back. He wore a Sergio Tichini sweat suit with the jacket of the sweat suit zipped down half way, revealing gold chains and a hairy chest.

"How are you doin Mr. Merlino? I hope I'm not disturbing you," Bobbi said timidly.

"No…have a seat," Merlino said, pulling a chair out for Bobbi. Bobbi sat down in the seat as she watched the mob boss stuff a fat cigar in his mouth.

"Well I won't take up too much of your time. I just wanted to talk about your lawyer, Emani Cooper", Bobbi said, as she sat on the opposite side of the table, across from the mob boss.

"What about her?" Merlino asked, blowing cigar smoke out of his mouth.

"Well, I know she doesn't have your best interest at heart."

"Yeah, how would you know this?" Merlino asked as he plucked ashes from his cigar into an ashtray.

"Well I'm an acquaintance of Miss Emani Cooper and she told me a lot."

"Well tell me more." Bobbi told Merlino various information about Merlino that she shouldn't have known. The sort of details that were attorney/client priviledged.

In the past, Emani had told Bobbi detailed information about the Merlino case. Emani hadn't thought that Bobbi would one day use that information against her. Bobbi lied and exaggerated details, but had Merlino convinced that she was being truthful.

"So why are you tellin' me all this?" Merlino asked.

"I'm telling you this because I don't think it's right for her to lose your case on purpose. She used the terminology of you being an animal, but I know you're just a human being."

In truth, Bobbi was the one who thought Merlino was an animal.

"I still don't understand, why are you tellin me this? You say you don't think it's right for her to lose my case on purpose, but that's bullshit. Everybody has an angle, so what's yours?" Merlino asked, rolling the cigar between his fingers.

"I don't want anything for this information. Just knowing I can sleep good at night is enough for me."

"I can respect that. You don't have too many honest people left out in this cold and cruel world. People would want money or something for this information you are providing me. I thank you though and if you need anything at all please let me know. You know where to find me." Merlino stood up to give Bobbi a handshake.

"Your welcome." Bobbi accepted the gesture and shook Merlino's hand.

Bobbi gave Merlino a smile and started walking out of the restaurant.

"Joey, show the pretty lady out." Merlino said to his muscle bound goon.

Bobbi took in the biggest breath she ever took when she walked out of the restaurant. Then a big smile started to form on her face.

"Yeah Emani, pay back's a bitch," Bobbi thought as she sat in her car feeling better already.

"So what do you think?" one of Merlino's goons asked, between bites of his spaghetti.

"I think she's tellin the truth. She knew too much information, information only me and my lawyer suppose to know about." Merlino said, puffing on his cigar.

"So what do you wanna do about it?" Merlino's goon asked.

"What do I wanna do about it? I want this monkey bitch

lawyer of mine wearing cement shoes at the bottom of the Delaware River. You hear me? That bitch that just left has to go too. She knows too much." Merlino said, with a killer's look in his eyes.

"Damn shame them two fine ass mully bitches gotta get whacked. I wanted to get a blow job from them," another one of Merlino's associates said as he openly rubbed his crotch.

Bobbi sat outside in her Infinity Q45 with her head leaned back against the headrest. Bobbi had no idea that she just signed her and Emani's death warrant.

"Emani is going to learn not to mess with me. Damn I would love to be there to see her face when that mob animal tells her she's fired. I know the cheatin bitch better not come running to me." She thought.

Bobbi started up her Q45 and drove off with a devilish look on her face.

CHAPTER 18

"Hello."

"Baby are you almost ready? The plane is leaving in about two hours." Skeam said on the other line.

"I think so, I just don't want to forget anything," Stori said as she looked around her room.

"Don't worry bout dat. We going shopping once we get down there anyway," Skeam said, looking at his Breitling wrist watch checking the time.

"We better be going shopping when we get there," Stori said, smiling on the other end of the line.

"Yes, shop-a-holic we're going shopping. That is if you ever get ready."

"Ok then, mister rush me man. Come on and get me."

"I'll be there in twenty minutes...holla!"

Stori had broke down months ago. She knew she broke her number one rule by letting Skeam know where she lived. But Stori realized when it came to Skeam that she was also breaking rule number two, three, four, five, six, seven, eight, nine and ten. Her house phone rung again just as she closed her Louis Vuitton suit case.

"This boy better stop rushing me," Stori thought. Stori looked at her caller I.D. box. She quickly realized it wasn't Skeam calling. It was Zikeema calling for the thousandth time. Once again Stori decided not to answer it, letting her answering machine pick up instead.

BEEP!

"Damn, Stori…if I didn't know no better I would think you was ducking me. What's up? I've been trying to get with you for a couple of days now. Me and Tori tryin to figure out what's the situation wit da rapper bul? You got us sittin in the dark and we ready to get this thing done. You know Tori needs this, so she can fall back and do the housewife thing. So do me a favor…if you can remember you got a sister give me a call back. Bye."

BEEP!

Stori felt guilty ducking her sisters and leaving them hanging. Stori knew her loyalty belonged to her sisters and she would do anything for them. She just found herself liking Skeam more and more each day they spent together. Stori tried to figure out a way that she could please her sisters, rob Skeam, and continue to see Skeam once the stick-up was over. Stori couldn't come up with a good plan. She was started thinking that maybe she didn't want to come up with a good plan. She knew sooner or later she would have to do something. Stori tried to clear her head but focused instead on sneaking off on a trip with Skeam.

"I see you are looking as good as ever," Skeam said as he loaded up her luggage in the car.

"Thank you for noticing," Stori said blushing a little.

"Girl, what you do bring your whole wardrobe?"

"Shoot, I wanted to bring some more stuff, but somebody was rushing me. I'm not gonna say no names though." Stori said, as she looked Skeam up and down with her lip twisted.

"You better hope they got room on the plane for all these bags you got here. If you would've brought one more bag, the plane probably would have been too heavy to make it off the ground." Skeam said, showing off his pearly whites.

"Now you want to be a comedian right?" Stori asked, standing with her hands on her hips.

"Naw baby, you know I'm just teasing you. Come here and give me a kiss." Skeam said as he took Stori in his arms giving her a deep passionate kiss.

"We're not going to make this plane if you keep kissing me like this," Stori said, pulling away from Skeam.

"We don't have to go. I'll cancel the trip right now," Skeam said, embracing Stori.

"Boy, stop playing before we be late," Stori said, pulling away again.

Skeam and Stori made it to the plane on time as they headed to the Virgin Islands.

"Baby, is everything alright? Since we got on this plane you haven't been yourself," Skeam said, as he looked into Stori's eyes.

"Uhmmm yeah...I'm fine. Why you ask me that?" Stori said to Skeam.

"You're usually more talkative, now it seems like you're a million miles away."

"I just was thinking about these two hair salons I'm trying to get off the ground."

Stori was still thinking about her sisters and how they wanted to rob Skeam. She was so confused about the whole situation. She was still unsure of what to do.

"Baby we're going on this vacation to leave all the stress, and things behind us. So if I'm not tihinking about my business, you can't be thinking about yours."

"Your absolutely right. I'll deal with all that stuff when we get back."

Stori and Skeam were filled with excitement when they landed in the Virgin Islands. Stori looked around like a kid in a toy store and thought everything was so beautiful. The people, the land, and the ocean were all beautiful. Stori swore that everywhere she looked she spotted the loveliest thing she ever saw.

"This is so beautiful."

"Yeah, I love it down here and I knew you would like it. Come on, let's get our bags." Skeam said, placing his arm around

Stori's shoulder.

"Baby is that our ride?" Stori asked as she looked at an all white stretch Mercedes Benz limousine.

The chauffeur standing in front of it held a sign in his hand that read Mr. and Mrs. Skeam.

"You know it ain't nothing but the best for you baby," Skeam said, leading the way to the limousine.

After the skycap loaded up all the luggage in the trunk of the limousine. Skeam thanked the skycap with a $50 bill as he and Stori climbed in the back of the limousine.

"So how far is the hotel from here?" Stori asked as she snuggled next to Skeam.

"Where we're staying is only about a twenty minute ride from here. So sit back and enjoy the scenery."

Stori sat back looking at the beautiful sites. She couldn't help but feel a little guilty. Being as though she was suppose to be robbing Skeam, not enjoying beautiful things with him. After all, Skeam has been good to her from day one.

"Girl, just enjoy yourself while you're here. You can deal with the other nonsense when we get back to Philly," Stori thought for the hundredth time.

Twenty-five minutes later, Stori looked around and there wasn't a hotel in site.

"I thought you said the hotel was only twenty minutes away. All I see is a few beautiful homes." Stori said as she looked around for the hotel.

"I never said anything about a hotel," Skeam said smiling.

"Well, where are we suppose to be staying," Stori asked, giving him a dumb look. "Right here." They pulled up to a villa that sat on the beach.

"Skeam, are we staying here for real? This is beautiful," Stori said, looking at the villa that was made out of all glass.

"Do you really like it?"

"Do I like? I love it. I mean, you can actually look through the entire house."

The chauffeur guided the limousine through a long winding driveway. Once they reached the house, Stori's breath was taken away. "It looks like the house is sitting in mid air," Stori said, looking for beams or some other support structures.

"I call this the magic house. It gives you the illusion that the house is floating in mid-air."

"What's supporting the house to make it sit in mid-air?"

"What magician do you know that reveals his magic?" Skeam stood behind Stori and wrapped his arms around her.

"Boy, is this magic house safe?" Stori asked as she rubbed Skeam's forearms.

"Baby, I would never cause you no harm, and yes this house will have you safer than a baby in its mother's womb."

"Well lead the way to this magic house my Prince".

Skeam led Stori over a small bridge that took them to the front door. Through the glass, Stori could see the inside of the house was just as magnificent as the outside. Stori knew right away that the interior decorator had put a lot of thought into designing the inside of the house.

"This is lovely," Stori said, walking into the house.

The marble floors, furniture, chandeliers, and everything else in the house were shipped from Italy.

"I've never seen a house so beautiful"

"You mean villa," Skeam corrected Stori.

"Excuse me, Mr. Proper," Stori said, looking at Skeam with her hands on her hips.

"Girl let me show you the rest of the house…I mean villa," Skeam said, as he and Stori started laughing.

After Skeam showed Stori the entire house he finally showed Stori her room.

"This is your room, do you like?" Skeam said as he opened up the door to a spacious room.

"This is nice."

"I'm glad this is suitable enough for you. Make yourself at home and the chauffeur will bring your bags up shortly."

"I sure will make myself at home." Stori dove onto the huge round bed. Skeam smiled to himself proud to see that Stori was happy.

"Where is your room?"

"My room is right next door."

"So you're going to leave me in this big ol' bed by myself?" Stori asked as she rolled off her back and onto her stomach to look at Skeam.

"You don't have to be in this big bed by yourself," Skeam said as he sat on the edge of the bed.

"If I get lonely at night, maybe I'll bang on the wall for you to come over." Stori suggested as she crawled up next to Skeam placing her head on his lap.

For the past couple of months Skeam and Stori have engaged in heavy kissing and touching. Stori always stopped things once it started to get too heated. As she laid there with her head on Skeam's lap looking into his eyes, she felt that this may be the trip where she would finally make love to Skeam. Skeam had already taken Stori to Cancun, Cali, Jamaica, and Vegas. Skeam was such a gentleman on every trip they took together. He never pressured Stori into having sex. Now Stori was tired of Skeam's gentleman act. She was ready for Skeam to pull her hair while he was hittin it from the back. Stori knew that having sex with Skeam could only result into one of two things. If the sex wasn't worth a dime, she could get back on her job setting Skeam up. But if the sex was so good where Stori was reaching for things that weren't there, then she knew there would be more confusion in her life. Either way, Stori was ready to take that next step.

"So you're laying in this bed like you're sleepy. What, you ready to take a nap or something?" Skeam said playing in Stori's hair.

"Boy I'm full of energy. I don't need a nap. Matter fact, I'm ready to do something to get my adrenalin pumping. Do you think you can handle that?" Stori asked, sitting up.

"I got a little something down in the garage but I'm not sure if you can handle it."

"What did I tell you about underestimating me? You gonna mess around and get yourself embarrassed," Stori said. Skeam smiled already knowing how competitve Stori would react.

"Aight, put on some jeans and a t-shirt and meet me downstairs. Oh, and don't wear none of them high heels you always wearing. Put some sneakers or Timbs on."

Skeam sat in the kitchen eating fresh cherries waiting for Stori. He looked at the kitchen's clock and realized 40 minutes had passed.

"Why do women take so long to get ready for?" Skeam thought as he spit out a cherry seed into a napkin.

"You waiting on me?" Stori asked as she appeared in front of Skeam out of nowhere. Skeam looked at Stori and was unable to speak.

"Baby what's wrong? Why your tongue hanging out your mouth like that?"

"Oh, I'm good." Skeam said, standing up from his chair.

Stori stood in the middle of the kitchen wearing a pair of Dolce and Gabbana jeans and belly shirt, and a pair of Nike Air Jordans that matched her outfit perfectly.

"You look tastey baby."

"What, this old stuff," Stori said, staring down at her clothes.

"This don't look old to me," Skeam said, snatching a price tag off Stori's shirt.

"Oooops, how did I forget that tag?" Stori asked a bit embarrassed.

"I don't' know, but you might be dressed a little too sharp for what we are about to do.

"Well what are we about to do anyway?" Stori asked as she grabbed a cherry out of Skeam's bowl.

"It's a surprise," Skeam said, pulling Stori close for a hug.

"Well this is the most casual outfit I got. So this will have to do." Stori said, giving Skeam a peck on the lips. "In that case, follow me."

They walked over the bridge around the side of the house to a five-car garage that was detached from the magical villa.

"You sure you're ready for this?"

"Bring the noise." Stori said confidently.

Skeam smiled at Stori then hit a button on the garage remote. One of the five garage doors opened revealing two Banshee 350 Twin four wheelers.

"Oh, these are cute," Stori said as she ran her hand across the four wheeler.

"You know anything about these?" Skeam asked Stori as he climbed onto one of the four wheelers and sat down.

"Well, I've seen the young guys around my way riding these things." Stori said as she climbed onto the other four wheeler.

"Well look, I'm a give you a quick crash course on how to ride these babies," Skeam said, getting off his four wheeler and walking over to Stori.

"Ok daddy," Stori said in her baby voice.

"The first thing I want you to know is your brakes are all on the right side of the four wheeler. Right here where your right foot is, is your brake. Where your right hand is, is your front brake. Remember that, I don't want you crashing into anything."

"Ok daddy." Stori said again in her baby voice as she batted her eyelashes.

Skeam continued to teach Stori how to ride the four wheeler. He showed her everything she needed to know about riding a four wheeler.

"You think you ready to ride?"

"I think so, Daddy." Stori put on her helmet, gloves, and her pair of goggles. Skeam did the same thing as they both started the four wheelers.

"I'm a ride behind you until I think you got the hang of it!" Skeam yelled over the loud Banshee four wheelers.

Stori shook her head and smiled as she slowly drove out of the garage. Skeam followed behind Stori down to the sand. Stori looked back at Skeam making sure he was directly behind her. When she was satisfied, Stori let her clutch halfway out, then pressed hard on the thumb throttle. Sand sprayed all over Skeam. After she sprayed Skeam, Stori performed five doughnuts in the sand before taking off at top speed down the private beach. Then she popped a wheelie.

After shaking the sand off of himself, Skeam took off after Stori. Skeam couldn't believe Stori could ride better than him. He desparately tried to keep up. Stori drove circles around Skeam for an hour or so before they both rode down to the water and turned off their four wheelers.

"That was fun," Stori said, taking off her helment and goggles."

"Yeah I bet, why you didn't tell me you knew how to ride like that? You were out there looking like you was part of the Ruff Ryders." Skeam said after he took off his helment and goggles.

"You never bothered to ask me if I knew how to ride. You just assumed I didn't know how. So I just let you assume that."

"You're right and I'm sorry for assuming."

"I accept your apology but I did warn you about underestimating me" Stori said, as she knocked some sand off her jeans.

"Never will I underestimate you again in life. Now, are you ready to ride some more?"

"I still want to ride. I'm just hot and thirsty. I know you're thirsty too with all the sand I was kicking up in your face." Stori said smiling.

"Ha, ha, ha…I see you got jokes. Let's go put these four wheelers up. I got something else for you to ride."

"Are you getting fresh with me?"

"Not yet, but this ride you'll need your bikini for."

Skeam and Stori rode the water on his jet skis for the next two hours.

"I don't know when the last time I had this much fun." Stori said as she and Skeam brought the jet skis back to the dock.

"I know, we were like two little kids out there," Skeam said, helping Stori onto the dock.

"We were out there acting crazy weren't we?" Stori asked as she pulled a wedgie out of her butt. "That was you acting crazy. So what your crazy butt ready to do next?" Skeam asked as he and Stori walked back to the magical house.

"I can honestly say that all the energy I'm usually full of, you drained every bit of it. I'm just ready to clean up and relax."

"That sounds like a good idea. That way, tomorrow I can show you the island and we can do your favorite pass time... shopping." Skeam placed his arm around Stori's waist.

"Goodie," Stori said cheerfully, clapping her hands together.

Stori and Skeam used their private bathrooms to get washed and dressed. Skeam was finished first. He came out wearing a linen short set and some flip-flops. As usual, Stori took extra long. When she finally managed to get dressed Stori came out wearing a bikini top and a pair of shorts that would make Daisey Duke feel naked. On her feet she wore her favorite bunny slippers. Stori walked out onto the patio carrying a book in her hand. She walked up behind Skeam pinching his butt.

"Girl, I didn't even hear you walk up. Are you hungry?" Skeam asked, pouring charcoal in a barbecue grill.

"I'm starving, but please don't burn the house down."

"Please girl, I could open up a five star restaurant with my cooking skills." Skeam picked up the lighter fluid.

"I'll be the judge of that." Stori curled her feet under her as she sat down in an oversized cushioned chair.

"What you reading?"

"Nicolette's book *Paper Doll*." Stori said, showing Skeam the book.

"Yeah, I heard that was an excellent book. Let me see that when you're done."

"Nope, go out and buy your own. You of all people should know that we have to go out and support our people. Especially a sister from our hometown Philly."

"You're absolutely right. I know I hate for a nigga to bootleg my shit and pass it around. When everybody could've went out and copped their own copy. " Skeam said as he took a sip of his Heineken.

"Well you make sure you go out and buy yourself a copy of this book."

Stori leaned back in her chair and started reading.

"I will, but until then, I'm a go up in here and grab these steaks for the grill," Skeam said as he disappeard into the house.

Skeam continued to cook while Stori read deep into her book.

"Baby, can you help me move this big ol' chair around? This sun is starting to blind me." Stori said, blocking the sun's glare with her hand. "Wait, you don't have to move." Skeam announced, grabbing a remote from off the table. "Boy, wait for what? You see the sun is starting to go down and the glare is blocking my vision." "Didn't I tell you this was the magical house?" Skeam hit the remote control. When he let the button go the house started to rotate. Stori couldn't believe what the house was doing. The back of the house rotated all the way around to where the front of the house once sat. Stori had a whole new scene to view. "I can't believe what just happened. I know this house didn't just move." "Well you said you wanted the sun out of your eyes and as you already know, your wish is my command." Skeam said as he waved his arms around in the air. "You are something else, you know that?" Stori said, getting up to give Skeam a kiss.

After Skeam and Stori ate their steak, baked potato, string beans, and tossed salad, they both sat back sipping Courvoisier.

"Thank you for bringing me here. This whole place is so beautiful." Stori said, babysitting her glass of Cognac. "It's not more beautiful than you," Skeam admitted as he rubbed his had across Stori's face. "If you think I'm so beautiful, why aren't you kissing me right now?" Stori asked as she placed her drink on the table. Without saying a word, Skeam passionately kissed Stori sliding his tongue between Stori's soft lips. She returned the gesture by placing her tongue into his mouth. After ten minutes of heavy kissing and touching, Skeam anticipated finally feeling Stori's insides. "Baby I think I'm ready to go upstairs," Stori said as she tried to catch her breath. "Well here, let me help you."

Skeam scooped Stori up into his arms and carried her upstairs. Skeam walked into Stori's room and gently laid her down on the bed. "Can you stay in here with me tonight?" Stori asked, looking up at Skeam. "Yes, I can do that." "Well come here then." Skeam bent down and Stori started undressing him. When Skeam was completely naked, he started to undress Stori. Skeam slowly removed Stori's clothes piece by piece. Skeam began kissing Stori all up and down Stori's naked body. "I want you inside me," Stori whispered in Skeam's ear. Skeam reached in the nightstand drawer and pulled out a condom. After securing the condom on his penis, he slowly climbed between Stori's legs and kissed on her neck. Before entering Stori, Skeam grabbed the remote to turn on the stereo. Luther Vandross' soulful voice crooned through the speakers. Skeam slowly entered Stori. Stori bit her bottom lip and held Skeam tight. She loved how Skeam felt inside her. Three hours and forty minutes later Stori and Skeam were soaked with sweat. She still couldn't believe Skeam sexed her in positions she never knew existed. It was official. She was in love with Skeam. Stori never had anyone make love to her as good as Skeam. Now she laid there with her head on Skeam's chest thinking, "What am I gonna do about my sisters?"

CHAPTER 19

With her car parked in her garage, Diamond stepped out
ready to take her clothes and high heels off. All that she could
think about was a hot bath with bubbles. Before she got a chance
to shut her car door a dark figure grabbed her from behind.
Diamond kicked, punched, scratched, and wiggled struggling to
get out of the intruder's grip. Diamond realized her struggle was
useless. The person behind her was entirely too strong.

"Bitch calm down before I kill you," the intruder said as he
placed a rag over Diamond's mouth.

The rag was soaked with some kind of strong chemical that
Diamond never smelled before. Diamond tried to pull the strang-
ers hand from her mouth, but her attempts were ineffective. The
chemical made her gag as she tried not to inhale it.

Diamond eventually passed out. The next thing she
remembered was waking up in bed. Diamond tried to rise but
realized her hands were tied down. She closed her eyes trying to
suppress the migraine headache she was experiencing. Diamond
opened her eyes again recognizing that her headache wasn't
going away. Fear then gripped her whole body. A man stood
next to her.completely naked except for the ski mask he wore
over his face. The masked man looked down upon Diamond
eating a sandwich. Diamond tried to scream but the duct tape
over her mouth muffled her cries.

"I see you're finally awake. I was waiting for you to join me.
I mean, fuckin you while you were passed out was wonderful.

So I know when I stick my dick back up in you, while you are awake, it's gonna be a special treat" the masked man said as he continued to eat his sandwich while rubbing and stroking his penis.

Diamond couldn't believe this was happening to her. She was always careful of her surroundings. She always made sure no one was following her. This time she wasn't careful enough.

The masked man finished his sandwich. He wiped mayonnaise off of his mouth before climbing onto the bed next to diamond.

"Temptation, don't be scared, I'm a gentle man."

Diamond knew then that the masked man knew her from the go-go clubs.

"You are so beautiful, you know that?" He ran his fingers through Diamond's hair. Diamond laid there helpless with fear in her eyes.

The masked man stuck his tongue out through the slit in the mask, and started licking Diamond all over her face. Diamond moved her head from side to side trying to block all the licks. Eventually Diamond stopped moving when she realized that all the motion was causing more saliva on her face. After five minutes of face licking, the masked man started to move down towards Diamond's breast. Before she knew it, her nipple was in his mouth. This was the first time Diamond realized she was completely naked. Tears started to roll down the side of her face as she awaited her fate. After another ten minutes of having her nipples licked, the masked man moved even further down Diamond's body. Diamond started to panic once she realized what the masked man was about to do. Kicking and wiggling, she tried desparately to remove the masked man off of her.

Within seconds her struggling stopped. The masked man held a butcher's knife to Diamond's stomach.

"Now we can do this the hard way or the easy way."

The masked man pointed the tip of the sharp knife at Diamond's belly button. Diamond know she could'nt win so she let her body go limp. The masked man spreaded Diamond's legs apart and dove inside her with his tongue. He licked and sucked on Diamond's clit. Her entire body went numb. Diamond felt like the masked man's face was down there for an eternity. He spent eight minutes performing oral sex on Diamond.

"I wish you could go down on me, but I don't trust you. I would have to kill you if you bit my dick off." The masked man rose from in between Diamond's legs, wiping his mouth. Diamond laid there thinking. She wished he would try to stick his dick in her mouth because she would definitely bite it off.

Diamond watched the masked man as he got up with the knife in his hand. He used his other hand to stroke his already erect penis. Diamond's eyes widened with fear watching the masked man climb between her legs. "Don't worry, I'm clean." Diamond's eyes shifted back and forth between the sharp looking knife and the condomless penis. She didn't know which one scared her the most. Once the masked man entered Diamond, she started to fight. She quickly realized that her fighting made the masked man more aroused and caused her more pain. So she tried to take her mind to a different place as the rapist handled his business.

The masked man continued to pound away at Diamond's insides sweating all over her body. Ten minutes later, Diamond felt a load of his sperm explode inside her. She wanted to throw up, but was afraid that the duct tape covering her mouth would make her drown in her own vomit. The masked man finally rolled off of Diamond and lit a Newport cigarette. "Damn, it's hotter than a mutha'fucka in this mask. I wish I could take it off, but if I did, I know I would have to kill you." Diamond laid there in shock as she thought to herself, "Maybe killing me wouldn't be all that bad."

For the next five hours, the masked man continued to rape Diamond over and over again. The only image Diamond had in her mind was a heart with a knife protruding from it. This was the same image tattooed on the masked man's right forearm. As long as she lived, Diamond knew she would never forget that tattoo. Diamond looked up and the masked man was completely dressed. "I wish I could stay longer, but I have to go. I had a really good time though." The masked man bent down and kissed Diamond on her forehead. Diamond laid there with a blank look on her face. "You don't have to say anything, I know you'll miss me." The masked man laughed and stood up straight. He left Diamond's bedroom laughing all the way to the front door.

Diamond laid in her bed motionless for another three hours. She still couldn't believe what had just taken place. She asked God over, and over again was he punishing her for dancing. "My sisters was right, what was I thinking of, being an exotic dancer. I could have been anything." Diamond thought. Diamond layed there for another 45 minutes before she stopped feeling sorry for herself. Her survival skills started to kick in. "Shit…if nobody starts missing me, I could starve to death laying here." Diamond thought. Then fear gripped her body again as she thought, "What if the rapist comes back?"

Diamond began moving around trying to free herself. She felt her foot come across something cold and hard that rested at the bottom of her bed. Rubbing her feet across the cold and hard object, Diamond realized it was the masked man's butcher knife. She carefully maneuvered the knife between her feet. Once the knife was secured, she brought the knife up to her awaiting hand. She proceeed to cut the ropes that had her wrist bound. Diamond feverishly cut through the ropes until her hands were free. Before she knew it, she stood in the shower under scalding hot water. She scrubbed her body with soap over and over until her skin felt raw. Diamond sanitized her body and unleashed a pool of tears in the shower. Eventually, Diamiond stepped out and dried off.

She put on her fluffy terry cloth bathrobe and placed her .38 caliber handgun inside the robe's pocket. Diamond checked all the doors and windows to make sure that they were locked. She sat down with a cup of herbal tea to think hoping to clear her head. "I can't tell nobody what happened to me," Diamond thought. She knew she could tell her sisters and they would support her and show love. Yet, Diamond did not want to hear her sister's saying "I told her so" behind her back. She didn't want pity from no one. So she decided to keep everything to herself. One thing was for sure, she would not let the masked man get away with what he'd done to her. She would make it her business not to rest until she found out who raped her. If she found out who raped her, she would try to kill him more than once, if that was actually possible.

CHAPTER 20

"Girl, get da fuck off me!" Ishmael said to Zikeema as he pushed her off of him.

"What's wrong baby? You didn't like the way I was ridin you or something?" Zikeema asked while rubbing Ishmael's sweaty chest.

"What's wrong? What's wrong? I'm up in here making love to the woman I'm ready to spend the rest of my life with and you talkin 'bout some, 'Hhhmmmm Kyree, you feel so good. Who da fuck is Kyree, because it surely ain't me?"

Ishmael swung his legs over the side of the bed, got up, and started pacing back and forth. Zikeema's mind was clouded with confusion. She laid in the bed trying to remember if she actually called Ishmael, Kyree. She then realized that he had to be telling the truth because he didn't know Kyree.

Ever since the night Kyree saved her life and killed Big Tyme, Zikeema had been thinking about him every second of the day. Zikeema knew she was in love with Ishmael but she got really wet every time she thought of Kyree.

"Oh, da cat got your muthafuckin tongue or something? No... no...hold up, Kyree got your muthafuckin tongue, right? Damn, I don't believe you called me some other niggah's name. Fuck it though. I hope you and Kyree have a happy life together, because, I'm out." Ishmael said, grabbing his clothes and putting them on.

"Wait baby, let me explain," Zikeema said, reaching out

trying to stop Ishmael from putting on his clothes.

"What? Explain! Ain't no more rap. I tried waiting on you to come around. Now it's time to do me." Ishmael said. "I'm not gonna continue to be your door mat, so you can keep wiping your feet on me. I'm tired of you thinking I'm a sucka." Ishmael continued as he slid on his wheat colored Timberland Chukka boots.

"I'm sorry baby. Can we talk about this? Just don't get up and leave like this." Zikeema said as she sat naked in the middle of the bed.

"You right, you is sorry. Too sorry to be with me," Ishmael said, walking out of the front door.

Zikeema sat there with her face cupped in her hands.

"Damn, what am I gonna do with myself?" Zikeema thought as she sat on her bed contemplating what she needed to do with her life. She thought about how she slipped up and called Ishmael out of his name. Through out their entire relationship, Zikeema never cheated once on Ishmael. But Zikeema had been spending a lot of time with Kyree ever since that fateful night when her life flashed before her eyes.

Zikeema loved everything about Kyree. She loved how Kyree was so spontaneous and always unpredictable. She also loved how freaky he was in bed. Yet, she felt guilty all the time for betraying the trust that she and Ishmael held for one another. Now she had let the cat out of the bag.

Ring...ring...ring!

The phone brought Zikeema out of her stupor. At first she wasn't going to answer it. Then she rushed to pick it up hoping that it was Ishmael calling to make up.

"Hello!"

Zikeema grabbed the phone expecting to hear Ishmael's voice.

"Girl, what you doin?" Tori asked on the other line.

"Oh, it's you," Zikeema said as the excitement in her voice

deflated.

"Well thanks for making me feel so special," Tori pouted.

"Tori, I'm sorry. I'm just goin through some men drama right now."

"You wanna talk about it?"

"Naw, I'm good, what's up wit you though?"

Zikeema got out of the bed and slipped on her robe.

"You know what's up, getting that niggah Skeam is what's up." Tori said, starting to lose her patience with the delay of the robbery.

"Oh, it's on…with or without Stori. I've been doin my home-work and this niggah is gonna be sweet. He's the only star I know that doesn't keep a lot of bodyguards around him." Zikeema said as her depression started fading away. "Usually he's by himself so we can hit 'em hard and be out before anybody knew we were even there."

"So what about Stori? Should we tell her that we're going to do this without her?" Tori asked.

"Hell no! We not telling that huzzy nothing. She left us hanging all this time. I just wanna see her face after me and you come up on this niggah and we countin millions in front of her face. I know she's going to want a breakdown, but she's not getting a dime from out of my cut." Zikeema said, picturing herself laying naked in bed all over Skeam's money.

"I know, right? She's been shittin on us for the past few months. I haven't really seen her or nothing. But I tell you what, after this come up, I'm done. Jerome's ass is starting to get too damn suspicious."

"Shit girl, how you think he's going to be acting when you bring Skeam's cash in the house?"

"Look, I'm a drop all that shit on the table and tell him the truth. I'll then let him know, I'm done with that lifestyle." Tori said with a serious voice. "So he can either except my pass or leave me and the kids alone."

"Tori, who you think you talkin too? I'm your sister not some stranger. You know damn well you not letting your husband go no where."

"Girl, you right about that. I'll shoot that niggah in both his knee caps before I let him walk out that door."

"Ha! Ha! Ha!...Tori you crazy. It's a damn shame that that man got you sprung like that and it's a bigger shame that deep down I know you're serious.

"Hmmmm, think I'm not?" Tori said, letting Zikeema know she wasn't playing.

"Anyway crazy...you talk to Diamond lately?" Zikeema asked.

"I called her the other day to see if she wanted to go on this mission with us, but she said she was cool. I don't know what's goin on with her. All I know is she's been acting real strange lately."

"I know, I called her the other day too and she was acting all weird. I think her ass is pregnant or something." Zikeema said.

"I don't know but I'm a make it my business to find out what's going on with my baby sister," Tori said.

"When you find something out you make sure you let me know too." Zikeema said, just as much worried about Diamond as Tori.

"So when are we going on this mission?" Tori asked, rubbing her hands together with anticipation of handling her business.

"I want to hit 'em next weekend. I already got all of the supplies and stuff that we're going to need. All we gotta do is go over the plan and we in there, like last year."

Zikeema was proud that she did all the planning by herself.

"Aight that'll work. I'm ready to get this done and over with." Tori said.

"Girl, we ready to get paid for real," Zikeema said hyped.

"Boy, I'm a break your neck, get your ass off of that table," Tori yelled.

"Who you talkin to like that?"

"Your bad ass nephew. He's starting to get too damn grown for himself. I see I'm a have to beat his ass in a minute." Tori said, taking off her belt and laying it across her lap as she stared at her son.

"You better not touch my nephew. Put my little man on the phone." Zikeema told Tori.

"J.J. get over here, boy come her. I'm not going to hit you. Your Aunt Zikeema wants to talk to you." Tori said handing her son the phone.

"Hiwo.., hi aunt Keem-Keem."

"Hi little man. What you doing over there, being bad?"

"No Aunt Keem-Keem...I wa...I wa tryin to get Lady's Barbie doll of da table for her," J.J. said, talking like a true five year old.

"Oh, you was trying to be a good big brother?" Zikeema asked her favorite nephew.

"Ycs, I'm a big boy," J.J. said proudly.

"Well keep being a good big brother and I'll be over there to pick up you and your brother and sister. Where do you want to go?" Zikeema asked J.J.

"Da zoo Aunt Keem-Keem. I wanna see da gorwillas at da zoo." J.J. said, ready to go to the zoo that second.

"Okay, just keep being a good big brother and I'll be over there tomorrow to take ya'll to the zoo."

"Yeaaah, we goin to da zoo, we goin to da zoo," an excited J.J. said dropping the phone to the floor forgetting to say bye to his aunt.

"Zikeema, why you got this boy doing cartwheels in my living room like he lost his damn mind?" Tori asked, watching her son do flip after flip like he had no sense at all.

"Leave my baby alone. I told him I was taking him, Chewy and Lady to the zoo tomorrow. So have them ready to go by noon."

"How you know I didn't have plans for them already?"

"Because I know you're goin to have them stuck in the house while you watch them ignorant stories of yours," Zikeema said with her nose turned up. "Yeah, tomorrow will be perfect for them to get out the house, because Luke and Laura is acting a fool on General Hospital and I'm a need some peace and quiet around here," Tori said, happy the kids would be out of the house while her stories were on.

"I'm not tryin to hear about them ig'nant stories. Just have my babies ready,"

"Shit, they bad asses will be dressed and ready tonight. So when they wake up, I can just push 'em straight out the door." Tori said with a serious voice.

"Didn't I tell you to stop messing wit my babies? You know I'll fight your crazy ass over them," Zikeema said, playing with her sister.

"Please, you know you could never beat me. I used to whip your ass, when we was little," Tori said, edging her sister on.

"Heffa, are you crazy? The only reason you would get over on me is because you and Stori would roll on me," Zikeema said, reminiscing on the good ol' days.

"If you don't stop lyin. We jumped you one time and that's because you was biting me on my back. Shit, I still got your teeth marks to prove it." Tori said, as she unconsciously rubbed her back where the teeth marks were located.

"Why you bringing up old stuff?" Zikeema asked not wanting to admit that her younger sister used to beat her up.

"I tell you what. Have your boots laced up tight when you get over here tomorrow. I'm a pull the gloves out so we can go a few rounds," Tori said, throwing out a left jab in front of her.

"No thanks, you not gonna have Stori hidin in the closet ready to jump out on me and besides, I don't think you'll be able to watch your stupid stories with two black eyes," Zikeema said as she and Tori shared a laugh.

"Girl, and you call me crazy. Let me get off of this phone so I can start dinner," Tori said.

"Yeah, I got to go too. I got this bad itch I need scratched," Zikeema said as she rubbed in between her legs.

"Bye nasty," Tori said.

"I love you too," Zikeema said, hanging up the phone.

Zikeema picked the phone back up and dialed a number. After three rings she got the voice she wanted to hear.

"Hi sexy, what's up?"

"Yeah, I miss you too," Zikeema said.

"I was hoping I could come over and get a fix," Zikeema added, using her sexy voice.

"Use your key to get in. I'll be waiting for you up in the bed." Kyree said, with a big Kool-Aid smile on his face.

CHAPTER 21

Stori was in a daze as she walked out of her doctor's office. She couldn't believe the news she received from her doctor. She vomited every morning for the past week. She thought that it was because of some Mexican food that wasn't agreeing with her stomach. Now she realized it was much more than that. Stori was two weeks pregnant? "I don't believe this shit. How can that be?" Stori thought, rubbing her stomach while she walked to her car.

Stori and Skeam had been sexually active with each other for the past five months. For the first three months she and Skeam used condoms faithfully. But for the last two months, the condoms came off. She felt secure about not using protection because they both took H.I.V. tests and Stori was getting Depo shots.

Now she was pregnant and confused. The pressure really was on for Stori. She was two weeks pregnant and her sisters were still putting the pressure on her to rob Skeam. She made up excuse after excuse about why it wasn't the right time to rob Skeam. She couldn't bring herself to tell them she was in love. Now this baby was going to force her hand into telling her sisters the truth.

"Why am I trippin? I'm ready to have a baby with the man I love," Stori thought. She began to think that she was betraying her sisters because she was sleeping with the enemy. "How did I get myself into this?" Stori asked herself as she got into her car. Stori always took pride in herself when it came to being in control. That's why she was always in charge of the stick-ups. Now she didn't know. She sat behind the wheel of her car crying, unsure if her tears were happy tears or sad tears. Contemplating what to do, Stori finally came to the conclusion that she should tell her sisters about everything.

Skeam had just got back in town from New York. He went to New York to take care of a few business matters and to do some shopping for Stori

"Yo Redz, you think Stori will like this?" Skeam asked his friend as he held up a fur coat.

"What? She gonna be all over that $50,000 Chinchilla," Redz said, wishing it was his.

"Yeah, this is a bad muthafucka," Skeam said, laying the sky blue and brown Persian lamb skin Chinchilla fur coat across his bed.

"So what's up? We goin to the club tonight or what?" Redz asked, rubbing his hands together and praying Skeam would say yes.

"Naw, me and Stori goin out tonight," Skeam said. Skeam smiled because he loved saying Stori's name.

Redz' face shown his obvious unhappiness. He didn't care for Stori too much because ever since she came into Skeam's life, Redz's party life slowed down drastically. Lately, Redz wasn't getting the left over groupies that he usually talked into having sex with him.

"You sure, Skeam? You know A.I. is having that party down club Egypt." Redz said, referring to the Philadelphia 76er's basketball star Allen Iverson.

"I don't care about that. I told you me and Stori is goin out. What part of that you didn't understand?" Skeam said a little agitated.

"That's cool, that's cool, I'll get wit you when you get back," Redz said quickly, noticing Skeam's attitude.

150

Once Redz left, Skeam washed and dressed himself so he could pick up Stori for their dinner date. Two hours later Skeam arrived at Stori's house. He rang her doorbell and waited.

"Hey sexy!" Stori said to Skeam when she opened the door

"You lookin more sexier than me. Look at you girl, you're glowin." Skeam said as he leaned in to give Stori a kiss.

Stori stood there blushing and unable to say anything.

"So are you gonna let me in or what?" Skeam asked, breaking her out of her trance.

"Oh, I'm sorry come on in." Stori stepped to the side to let Skeam pass.

"So where you been at all day? I've been calling you like crazy." Skeam said as he sat down on the love seat.

"You been calling me all day? Damn what you doin,s talking me or something?" Stori asked Skeam.

Skeam sat there for a second with a stupid look on his face.

"I was just concerned and..."

"Boy, I'm only playing with you. Stop being so serious and learn how to take a joke." Stori said laughing at Skeam.

"Oh, you got jokes huh? OK, Mrs. Richard Pryor, you got that one." Skeam said crossing his arms over his chest and poking out his bottom lip.

"I'm sorry baby, I was sleeping all day," Stori said as she sat on Skeam's lap and showered his face with kisses.

Stori told Skeam she was sleeping because she still wasn't sure how to tell him that she visited the doctor's office and that she was two weeks pregnant.

"I just was missing you baby and needed to hear your voice bad," Skeam said still pouting.

"Awww...you so sweet," Stori said as she started kissing Skeam again. Skeam didn't waste any time as he started twirling his tongue around in Stori's mouth. Stori let out soft moans while their hands were used to explore each other's body.

"Boy stop before we end up naked in here," Stori said, pulling

Skeam's hand from inside her pants.

"That sounds good to me." Skeam unbuckled his belt.

"Cut it out nasty. You know we got reservations and I'm hungry as hell." Stori said, getting up off of Skeam.

"Let's go then so we can come back here and you can give me my dessert," Skeam said, lightly smacking Stori on her butt.

"Boy, you so fresh."

"Oh…before I forget, this is for you," Skeam said, handing Stori a bag.

"For me? You know I love surprises." Stori accepted the bag from Skeam.

"Well open it up then," Skeam said, sitting on the edge of the loveseat with anticipation.

Stori opened the bag astonished by what she saw.

"This, this is beautiful" Stori managed to utter as she held up her new Chinchilla fur coat.

"I'm glad you like it," Skeam said, walking up behind Stori and hugging her.

"Baby, thank you, I love it." Stori turned around and gave Skeam a hug and kiss.

"Only the best for you boo," Skeam said smiling.

"Well you know what? Let's get to this restaurant. So we can get back and I can give you that dessert you just asked for," Stori said as she walked away seductively.

The restaurant was exquisite yet cozy with candles on all the tables. The hostess showed them to their table. Their waiter approached shortly afterwards with his pen and pad out ready to take their order.

"Let me get a double shot of Remy straight up and get her a double shot of Bacardi Limon with orange juice," Skeam said to the waiter.

"No, no, just get me a glass of water." The waiter took their orders and walked away.

"Boo you always drink Bacardi Limon. You not drinking

tonight?"

"No, I'm a leave the liquor alone for a minute," Stori said as she unconsciously rubbed her stomach.

"Is everything okay baby? You've been acting kind of distant tonight. Like you're in your own little world or something." Skeam said, reaching over the table to hold Stori's hand.

"I'm, I'm good. My sisters and I aren't seeing eye to eye right now that's all." Stori said unable to get her words together to tell Skeam she was pregnant.

"Well you know I'm here for you if you wanna talk about it," Skeam said as he looked into Stori's eyes.

"I know sweetie. I'm fine though."

Throughout the rest of their dinner Stori and Skeam weren't as playful with each other. Stori continued to think about how to tell Skeam the news of her pregnancy. With Skeam not understanding Stori's behavior, their dinner was unusually quiet.

"When are you gonna let me meet these famous sisters of yours anyway?" Skeam asked, attempting to break the tension.

"They've been wanting to meet you," Stori said knowing that their meeting wouldn't be a pleasant one.

"Well you have to set up a time when we all can get together."

"I'll do that," Stori said, thinking about the awkward encounter.

"How am I going to tell my sisters that I'm having a baby by Skeam and how can I tell Skeam that he is going to be a father." Stori continued in thought.

CHAPTER 22

FBI Headquarters in Philadelphia, PA

FBI Director Nicholas Smiley:

"This will go down today. Special agent Spagnetti will be purchasing one thousand black credit cards from our target Robert Whitehead, also known as Flea. Mr. Flea had been up and down the East Coast with his bad checks, fake credit cards, counterfeit money, and any other scam you can think of. He's left a paper trail a mile long and I want him bad. He walks with a severe limp from a shooting he sustained years ago. So there shouldn't be a problem with him trying to run away or anything. But as everybody should already know, still proceed with caution. I want this to go down quick and sweet. So everybody suit up and lets get this ball rolling." FBI Director Nicholas Smiley said as he debriefed his tactical unit.

*****

"Yeah, Becky. I'm supposed to be meeting the guy Mickey in another hour." Flea said, as he got dressed.

"How many cards is he buying?" Becky asked Flea as she sat in the front of the TV switching channels with the remote.

"He's buying a thousand of 'em," Flea said, yelling from the bedroom.

"Damn! And you are selling them for $500 a piece. That's half a mill you will make." Becky said with excitement in her voice.

"I know and this is what I need to put me in retirement. After this big score, I'm a pass everything over to Murk and let him and his team take over the business."

Flea walked into the living room where Becky sat.

"Are we still going to travel the world, daddy?"

"Baby as long as you're loyal to me, we'll travel the world twice. Now about this Mickey character. How does Vicky know him again?"

Flea never liked dealing with new people, but he couldn't let this opportunity get by him. Flea had been waiting for a one shot deal like this one. Little did he know, his worker Victoria, who was known as Vicky, got caught trying to use one of the fake credit cards. The Feds interrogated Vicky for four hours. They pressured her to confess by threatening that she would never see her one-year-old son again until he was twenty-one. Vicky finally broke. She agreed to set up Flea in exchange for leniency.

"He's Vicky uncle from Detroit. She said he sells hundreds of kilos of heroin a week up there. So he's supposed to be a real big time dude up Detroit."

Becky thought about the half million dollars Flea would soon have in his possession.

"Well as long as he shows me the cash there won't be a problem."

Flea stood in front of the mirror brushing his salt and pepper hair."

There shouldn't be a problem. I mean he can't beat the deal you are giving him."

"You damn right he can't beat that deal. He's spending $500 for each card that has a $10,000 limit. I say the muthafucka is robbing me." Flea turned to look a Becky.

"Relax daddy, everything will be OK." Becky said, getting up from the couch. She kissed Flea on the lips.

"I know. I'm just ready to get this done and over with. When that half mill is in my hands that's when I'll relax." Flea grabbed his car keys and walked out the door.

FBI Headquarters
"Now don't forget when you show him the money and he shows you the cards, take your hat off and scratch your head that will be our signal to move in." FBI director Nicholas Smiley said to agent Angelo Spagnetti.

"I got everything covered, don't worry about it." Spagnetti said.

Spagnetti placed his right hand on Smiley's left shoulder.

I know you'll do fine, that's why I specifically hand picked you for the job. I know everything will go smoothly. For the rest of ya'll, let's mount up and get ready to take down this scum bag."

*****

"So how do you suppose to recognize this Mickey guy?" Becky asked Flea as she drove to the meeting spot, a McDonald's parking lot at Broad and Diamond Streets.

"He told me he would have on a Detroit Lion's jacket and baseball cap, and he said he would be standing in front of his pearl Cadillac STS."

Flea reclined in the passenger seat of his Jaguar. He thought about the good run he had in the game. The game had been good to him and now was a good time to retire. Flea was 51 years old and had been in the game for 35 years. Out of all the pimps, drug dealers, number runners, bank robbers, and con artist he encountered over the years, Flea only knew of one guy that was able to retire out the game. Flea wanted himself as the second he knew that would retire out of the game. He wanted out before he got locked up or killed.

"Daddy, I want us to go to Paris first. You know I always wanted to go there." Becky said, also thinking about her retirement. "Baby whatever you want, we'll do," Flea said, lighting up a Black and Mild cigar. Becky wasn't in the game as long as Flea. For Becky, her 15 years in the game felt like 35 years. Becky loved Flea with all of her heart. She prayed for the day that Flea would ask to marry her. Becky was 36 years old and biological clock did more than just tick. It was ready to knock a door down.

"Daddy, I think that's him right there." Becky said.

She pulled into the McDonald's parking lot and pointed to a guy standing in front of a brand new Cadillac. He wore Detroit Lion's attire.

"Let's do this. Pull up and park right next to him." Flea said, rubbing his hands together while a Black and Mild cigar dangled in his mouth.

Murk casually walked up Broad Street stopping at a car parked directly across the street from McDonald's. He leaned inside the car window.

"Is everybody in position?" Murk asked his squad of young thugs.

"Yeah we all ready in here. We got Buck and Ham across the street on point posted up at the gas station. Wiz and Dink holdin shit down over at the McDonald's parking lot exit and I got Gee-man, Tron, and Mooney posted up inside the McDonald's. Anything crazy jump off, shit gonna be like the Wild Wild West out this bitch." Ty said to Murk as he sat in the car with Bird, Dog, and Lil Lamb.

"Aight, I see ya'll got the perfect view right here, so if you see any funny shit at all go down, move in wit ya'll guns blazin and everybody else will follow ya'll lead. Ya'll got it?" Murk asked everyone sitting in the car.

"Yeah, we got it," Ty, Bird, Dog, and Lil Lamb said in unison.

"Aight fam, ya'll keep ya'll eyes open." Murk said. He walked backed to his car that was parked nine cars behind Ty, Bird, Dog, and Lil Lamb's car.

"Baby stay in the car and keep it runnin, I'll be right back," Flea said, stepping out of the Jaguar. Flea walked with his cane in his right hand and a sneaker bag filled with a thousand fake credit cards in his left hand.

"So, you must be Mickey," Flea said as he switched his cane into his left hand so that he could shake Mickey's hand.

"That's me and you must be Flea," Spagnetti said, shaking Flea's hand.

"So how is it up in Detroit? I haven't been up there in years." Flea said, stealing a look at the parking lot.

"Motown is Motown, but I don't think we here to talk about my city."

"OK, OK, I see you are a man about his business."

"It's not like that, but I have a plane to catch in a few hours."

"I understand you got the money?" Flea took another look around.

"Step into my office."

Spagnetti led Flea to the trunk of his Cadillac. Spagnetti opened the trunk, revealing a black duffle bag. He unzipped the bag and bundles of money appeared.

"You wanna count it."

"Naw it looks straight to me. Besides Vicky's peoples is my peoples."

"Yeah, that's my favorite niece. Is that the cards?" Spagnetti asked, pointing to the sneaker bag in Flea's hand.

"No doubt, enjoy." Flea answered, handing over the bag of credit cards.

Spagnetti's heart started to pump fast as he grabbed the bag of credit cards from Flea. He always got a rush when he was about to take a criminal from off the streets. With some prior busts, he even got an erection when placing the handcuffs on the bad guys.

"Uhm, these are nice," Spagnetti said, as he took out one of the cards to inspect it by flipping it over and back.

"I'm glad you like 'em. Now if you can hand me that bag of money, we can finish this transaction and you can go and catch your plane." Flea said, holding his hand out.

Spagnetti wanted to play with Flea a little before he locked him up. Spagnetti thought, *"Let me give him this bag so that he can have a story for all the other low-lives in federal prison across the county. I can hear him now talking to his cell mate about how he had a half million in his hands before getting caught. His dumb ass will probably boost the sum up to whole million. Either way, this cripple is tasting his last bit of freedom."*

"Oh sure, here you go," Spagnetti said, handing Flea the Duffel bag.

"Good doing business with you," Flea said, turning and limping away.

"Oh Flea, one more thing." Spagnetti took his hat off and scratched his head.

"What's up?" Flea asked, turning around.

"FBI…FREEZE," Spagnetti yelled as he aimed his service revolver at Flea.

"I ain't goin to jail," Flea said. He looked back over his shoulder at Spagnetti.

Buc…Buc…Buc!

Becky stood out in front of the Jaguar squeezing the trigger of her .38 caliber hand gun. The first shot missed. The other two shots found their mark hitting Spagnetti in his neck and cheek. His FBI standard issue bullet proof vest could not protect Spagnetti from these bullets. Spagnetti dropped on the spot.

"Daddy, hurry let's go," Becky said with her .38 still in her hand.

Tat…Tat…Tat…Tat…Tat…Tat…Tat!

One of the members from the tactical unit pulled the trigger of his M-16 assault riffle. He hit Becky in the back of her shoulder causing her to spin around facing the person who shot her.

Buc..Buc..Buc!

Becky fired three more shots before she fell to the ground.

"Becky Noooo," Flea said.

Flea pulled out his .50 caliber Desert Eagle handgun and pulled the trigger. The armor piercing bullets of the Desert Eagle cut through the vest of the tactical team member. He dropped dead on the spot.

Flea advanced toward Becky's body. He was cut short by a barrage of bullets of the approaching tactical team members. Flea dove to the left behind special agent Spagnetti's parked Cadillac with all his strength while flying bullets missed him by inches. Just as the tactical unit was ready to come down on Flea, Gee-man, Tron, and Mooney came out of the McDonald's firing uzis with armor-piercing bullets.

Tat…Tat…Tat…Tat…Tat…Tat…Tat…Tat!

The tactical unit took cover. Gee-man came from the right side, Mooney came from the left, and Tron approached from the middle. With the extended clips on Gee-man, Tron, and Mooney's uzis, their shooting seemed endless.

"Yeah!!! I got one of those muthafuckas!" Gee-man yelled, as he watched one of the tactical team members fall to the cement. The rest of tactical team members took cover behind parked cars and a dumpster as bullets continued to fly. Wiz and Dink approached from the back of the parking lot boxing in the tactical unit.

"I need to get behind that car over there, so I can get a better shot," Mooney said. "Aight. I'll cover you," Tron yelled to Mooney.

Tron inched out from behind the wall to cover Mooney, but was shot instantly in the forehead. When Tron fell, Mooney realized that he was exposed without cover. As he tried to run behind a car for cover, one of the tactical unit members took careful aim and pulled the trigger. Pow! The bullet hit Mooney in the back of his head and exited through his left eye. His body crumbled on the asphalt.

"Damn," Gee-man said, realizing that he was now by himself.

Bullets started flying again. Shooting their way in from behind the parking lot were Wiz and Dink. The tactical team started returning fire. Ty, Bird, Dog, and Lil Lamb drove in from the opposite side of the parking lot as Wiz and Dink. They jumped out of their car. Lil Lamb started shooting first with a .45 caliber hand gun in each hand. He then took aim at the car that the tactical team used for cover. Lil Lamb's armor piercing bullets went through the driver's door and out the passenger's door. One tactical team member was hit in the ear with the bullet bouncing in his brain.

"Time to go out in a blaze of glory," Flea thought still holding his Desert Eagle in one hand and the bag of money in the other. While Flea's young thugs were working hard for him, in the back of his mind, he knew that the tactical unit's reinforcement would arrive any second along with every police district in the city.

They killed Becky, the love of his life, so he vowed to kill a few of them, before they took him out.

SCREEEEECH!!!

Flea turned aiming his gun toward the sound of screeching tires.

"Flea, it's me…let's go," Murk said.

He stopped his car next to Flea and opened the passenger door. Flea knew his top young thugs would come through for him.

"Here I come baby boy," Flea said rising from the ground.

Leaving his cane on the ground, Flea got up with his gun and the bag of money in hand. Flea stayed low as he limped towards Murk's car. Flea threw the bag of money in the car first.

"Let's go ol' head, we home free," Murk said smiling at Flea.

Flea smiled back and suddenly felt two sharp pains in his back. Two bullets hit Flea in the back knocking him inside the car. Murk reached over Flea's bent body and managed to shut the passenger side door.

Murk quickly escaped out of the parking lot, drove down Broad Street, and made a right onto Oxford Street.

"Ol' head, you aight?" Murk asked Flea, as he looked at all of the blood in the car.

Flea was unable to speak because of the pain shooting through his body.

"Just hold on Flea. I'm a get you some help," Murk said driving like a mad man.

A few minutes passed and Flea no longer seemed to be in pain. Actually he felt at peace. He looked over at Murk and couldn't help thinking about how 20 years ago he was driving and Big Toe sat wounded in the passenger's seat. "Déjà vu is a muthafucka," Flea thought. Flea died with a smile on his face knowing that he was about to see his long time friend, Big Toe.

CHAPTER 23

"Bobbi can we act like two adults and talk this out," Emani asked after calling Bobbi back for the fifth time.

"You gonna shit on me, then you want me to act like everything is normal between us. Bitch please!" Bobbi said sucking her teeth.

"Bobbi, I love you so I'm a look pass the name calling." Emani said with a sympathetic voice.

"I feel as though all this that's going on between us is just one big misunderstanding and if you'll just give us a chance to sit down with each other, I think we could work this out."

Emani never begged for anything in her life. Her pride wouldn't let her stoop that low. Now, with a torn relationship with Bobbi, Emani put her pride aside. She knew that she couldn't lose Bobbi. The several weeks that passed without Bobbi were torture for Emani. Losing Bobbi forever would devastate Emani. After all, Bobbi was her soul mate and Emani would fight to the end of time to get her soul mate back.

"You hurt me once Emani. You promised me you would never hurt me again." Bobbi said, crying over the phone.

"I'm sorry baby. Please let me make it up to you," Emani pleaded.

"Make it up to me, how?" Bobbi asked through her sniffles.

"Come on over my house and I'll think of something," Emani suggested with a seductive tone.

"No Emani, I don't want to come over there to have sex and then pretend that everything is supposed to be fine between us. If we are going to work this out we need to sit down somewhere and talk this out."

Bobbi tried to play hard to get, but was actually going crazy with not having Emani in her life.

"Well, you wouldn't be coming over here to have sex. You would be coming over to have great sex." Emani said attempting get Bobbi moist.

"Emani, I'm serious. If we are going to work on our relationship, we really need to talk."

"OK, you're right. Let's say we meet each other at Houlihan's in two hours."

"We can do that. I'll be there in two hours."

"Bobbi, I love you," Emani said before hanging up the phone.

Immediately following the phone call, Emani went to work trying to figure out what to wear to Houlihan's. Finally, after careful thought, Emani decided to wear her black Versace dress, which was Bobbi's favorite. Emani wanted to take a bath, but realized that she wouldn't have time to soak and gather her thoughts. Instead, she jumped into the shower. After her shower, she dried off and moisturized her body with Bath & Body Works blushing cherry blossom body lotion. Then she sprayed Gucci's *Envy Me* perfume on her neck and wrist, and between her thighs. Emani slid on her black Versace dress leaving her panties and bra in the drawer. She pulled her hair back leaving two curly strings of hair hanging down on both sides of her head. Her hair was damp giving it a wet look that highlighted her naturally curly hair. She put on her DKNY watch and a diamond necklace that Bobbi had bought for her on Valentines Day. She completed her outfit with a pair of Manolo Blahnik stilettos. Standing in front of the full length mirror Emani noticed her nipples getting hard. "Damn…I look good." She said as she admired her image. Emani applied her lip gloss, grabbed the keys to her Lexus GS, and left the house.

Bobbi made it to the restaurant first. After turning down advances from four different men, Bobbi sat there contemplating what she would say to Emani. She knew she wanted her and Emani to have a public relationship. She was tired of tip-toeing around for Emani. If they were in public and she wanted to hold Emani's hand, she didn't want Emani to snatch her hand back because people were staring. Bobbi didn't care about them other people. She only cared about Emani. Bobbi felt that if things were going to work out between them many changes were needed.

Bobbi spotted Emani walking in the restaurant and her breath was immediately taken away. "I see this hussy ain't playing fair already. She got my favorite dress on, looking all good and shit." Bobbi thought, as she continued to watch Emani sway towards their table.

"Hi!" Emani greeted, walking upon Bobbi's table with all of her pearly white teeth showing.

"Hi, yourself." Bobbi said as she stood up to give Emani a hug.

"Damn, she smells good," Bobbi thought while holding Emani in her arms.

"You're looking good," Emani said, taking a step back to look at Bobbi.

"Yeah, I see you are wearing my favorite dress. What are you tryin to do weaken my defense?" Bobbi said as she felt that special place between her legs become moist.

"Huh? I don't know what you are talking about," Emani said looking away, as she tried to play dumb.

"You don't know what I'm talking about? Yeah, OK." Bobbi answered.

Bobbi and Emani took their seats.

"Are ya'll ready to order?" the waitress asked with her pen and pad in hand.

"You can get me a White Zinfandel," Emani said, looking at

the menu."

"How about you ma'am?"

"I'll have the same thing." Bobbi answered.

The waitress took their remaining orders and walked off.

"It feels good seeing you," Emani said as she eyed Bobbi from across the table. "Yeah, it's good seeing you too...I think we should get straight to the problems." Bobbi suggested.

"I agree."

Emani sat back and crossed her legs. Bobbi began telling Emani how much she was tired of being secretive about their relationship. Bobbi went on about this dislike and that dislike. Emani sat quietly listening to Bobbi's concerns. When it was Emani's turn to speak, she agreed with Bobbi and promised that things would change. She told Bobbi about the day at Dave and Buster's. Emani explained that when she saw Bobbi she wanted to run into her arms. She mentioned that she was only giving the guy her number because he was a potential client. After an hour of agreeing with each other and making promises, they eventually reconciled with a kiss.

"It feels so good that we are back together," Bobbi said, holding Emani's hand from across the table.

"I know because I've been stressing lately," Emani said while taking a deep breath.

"Ahhh, did I have my baby stressing?" Bobbi asked, gently rubbing Emani's hand.

"Not only our situation, but for some unknown reason, Sammy Merlino, the infamous Philadelphia mob boss, fired me last week," Emani admitted with sadness in her eyes.

Before Emani mentioned him, Bobbi had forgotten her visit with Merlino. She sat across from Emani stuck on what to say.

"He, he did? Why did he say you were fired?" Bobbi asked.

"He wouldn't give me a reason. All I know is we had a scheduled appointment to go over a few things. When he came to the appointment he stuck his head in my office, said I was fired, and walked out. I tried to chase him down to find out what was he firing me for, but them big goons that he always has surrounding him had the nerve to put their hands on me, stopping me from talking to that damn 'chicken neck' Merlino. I know one thing, I'm a get to the bottom of this."

Emani looked off into space even more confused on why Sammy Merlino fired her. Bobbi clammed up fearing that Emani would never forgive her if she found out that Bobbi was behind Merlino firing her. Baby don't worry about it. I don't want you stressing yourself out over this. So why don't you look at it as it's Merlino's loss, not yours." Bobbi hoped Emani would agree and drop the subject.

"No, no, I'm a get to the bottom of this," Emani said with a determined look on her face. Bobbi felt herself starting to perspire, but remained quiet.

"Baby, I don't want to stress you out with my problems, so lets change the subject," Emani said.

Unable to do or say anything, Bobbi just smiled. The rest of their time at Houlihan's went smoothly. They both realized how much they missed each other. After Emani insisted on paying the bill, they both walked out together hand in hand.

"So what are you ready to do?" Emani asked rubbing Bobbi's cheek with the back of her hand.

"I got a few errands to run, then I'll probably just relax. Why do you ask?" Bobbi asked, lustfully eyeing Emani up and down.

"Because I got a surprise for you." Emani answered.

"What surprise? You know I like surprises."

"Well step into my car and I'll show you what your surprise is." Emani said as she unlocked her car door with the remote on her key chain.

When they reached the car, Emani sat in the driver's seat with Bobbi sitting beside her.

"So, where is my surprise?" Bobbi asked with excitement.

Emani took a quick glance surveying her surroundings. Once she felt that the coast was clear, Emani faced Bobbi by placing her back against the driver's door. Emani took another glance outside and focused her attention onto Bobbi.

"This is your surprise." Emani lifted her Versace dress with her legs apart revealing a perfectly trimmed love nest.

"Girl, you don't got no panties on," Bobbi said, loving the surprise.

"I don't have on a bra neither," Emani said, licking her lips.

"I already knew you wasn't wearing a bra. Your nipples was staring at me all through lunch. But you not having on no panties is definitely a surprise." Bobbi rubbed her hands between her own legs.

"Well do you lick it, I mean, like it?" Emani asked teasingly while spreading her legs even further apart.

"Do I like it? I love it, now can I play with my surprise?" Bobbi asked feeling her panty line getting wet.

"It's yours ain't it?" Emani expanded the lips of her vagina exposing her pink pearl.

With no hesitation Bobbi dove her hand in Emani's soak and wet pleasure box. Emani's head leaned back in ecstasy.

"Do you like that?" Bobbi asked Emani as she worked her magic with her hand.

"Uhhhmmm, I love it. You know that's my spot," Emani said, biting her bottom lip and looking lustfully at Bobbi.

"Damn, your pussy feels like silk."

Bobbi inserted two fingers inside Emani's vagina and used her thumb to rub Emani's clitoris. Bobbi used her other hand to reach into her own pants. Bobbi began rubbing Emani's clitoris faster anticipating that Emani would soon explode in her hand.

Right when Emani was about to have the best orgasm she had in a long time, Bobbi stopped.

"Please baby, don't stop, I'm about to cum," Emani moaned with her eyes closed.

A few seconds passed with no response from Bobbi. Emani opened her eyes confused about what was happening.

"Bobbi what's wrong?" Bobbi's eyes were filled with fear as she watched Merlino's muscle bound goon advance towards the driver's side of Emani's car. Intimidated by the size of the gun in the muscle bound goon's right hand, Bobbi was unable to think or react. Bobbi's fearful eyes caused Emani to look over her shoulder. As soon as Emani looked out of the driver's side window she saw the muscle bound goon raising his gun.

"Bobbi watch out!" Emani yelled, shielding Bobbi by throwing her body over Bobbi's body.

Boom...Boom...Boom...Boom...Boom...Boom...Boom! was the last thing Emani heard before everything went black.

CHAPTER 24

Ishmael still couldn't get over the fact that Zikeema betrayed their relationship as he drove around stressing over their break up. "How da fuck could she do me dirty like that?" Ishmael thought, as he inhaled a Dutch Master cigar filled with hydroponic marijuana. Ishmael was a thinker most of the time, but after the break up, Ishmael had been reckless. Usually Ishmael never touched any type of drug or alcohol, but ever since Zikeema called him out of his name, Ishmael hadn't been the same. Zikeema called him day and night, but Ishmael ignored her call every time. "Fuck it, I'm through with her. I'm tired of her thinking she can get away with treating me any way she wants." Ishmael thought, as he tried to psych himself out.

Deep down Ishmael knew that he was still madly in love with Zikeema. He wanted things to work out between them. He vowed to stand strong this time and not give in to Zikeema. Ishmael drove all around the city easing his pain with weed. He found himself in Southwest Philly driving down 52nd Street. He made a right onto Woodland Avenue and noticed a lot of cars and people were in front of Trendsetters, a local bar. "Let me slide up in here and see what's going on. Maybe I'll find my future wife in here since stinkin ass Zikeema wanna play games wit me." Ishmael thought while parking his Yukon Denali. Ishmael got out of his truck and walked towards Trendsetters. "Damn it's cold out this bitch," Ishmael thought, turning up the collar on his leather Pelle jacket and quickening his pace.

Once inside, Ishmael was glad he stopped in as he observed all the beautiful women in the bar. He unzipped his jacket and found a seat at the bar.

"What will it be handsome?" the barmaid asked.

"Well, I'm kind of embarrassed because I really don't drink. So I don't know what to order." Ishmael said, smiling at the dark skinned voluptuous barmaid.

"Well handsome, how about an apple martini? They're not that strong, but they'll sneak up on you." the barmaid said, bending over the bar giving Ishmael a full view of her cleavage.

"I'll take that if you'll let me buy you one and you'll drink with me." Ishmael pulled out a wad of money.

"Are you flirtin wit me?"

"As fine as you are, you think I'm not?" Ishmael answered staring at the barmaid's cleavage.

"Well I'm glad you are. My name is Terri by the way."

Terri couldn't help but think of all the sexual acts she would love to perform on Ishmael.

"I'm Ishmael."

"Well Ishmael, let me get us those drinks," Terri said, turning around so that Ishmael could see her fat round juicy ass.

"Damn that ass is fat. I'm a have to try and get that home wit me tonight." Ishmael thought, as the tight jeans Terri wore did its job.

Ishmael figured if Terri couldn't get Zikeema off his mind, nobody could.

"Here you go Ishmael and thank you for the drink."

"Hmmm, this is pretty good." Ishmael said as he sipped his drink.

"I figured you'd like it, but like I said, be careful with it. Since you're not a real drinker these Apple Martini's can sneak up on you."

Terri pulled a chair onto the opposite side of the bar and sat in front of Ishmael.

"If I do happen to get a little tipsy, you won't take advantage of me will you?"

"I'm hoping we both will get tipsy so we can take advantage of each other," Terri said, placing her black silky hair behind her ears."

"Well, in that case why don't you make us a big pitcher filled with this apple martini."

"I can do that." Terri said to Ishmael as she grabbed a big pitcher from behind the bar.

Terri sat back down so she could get to know Ishmael better. Terri and Ishmael became more comfortable with each other as they laughed, talked, and got drunk. Terri knew that if she had it her way she would have Ishmael in bed that night. She sensed that Ishmael was a great catch and she was determined to put her hooks in to him. The alcohol had Ishmael opening up. He talked about Zikeema and how she betrayed him. Terri sat there listening. She responded to everything Ishmael said, telling him everything that he wanted to hear.

"You're right. She don't deserve me. I don't know why I put up with her shit for this long." Ishmael said as his speech started to slur.

"Some women get a good man and don't know what they got. Me though, I keep my eyes open for good men, because they don't come along too often and I must say you are a good man. I know if I had you I would be home every day cooking a hot meal for you. I would run you a hot bath, wash your back for you, and cater to all your needs."

"Damn, all that? You gonna have me get on one knee right now and ask for your hand." Ishmael said as he and Terri shared a laughed.

"Boy is you gonna be able to drive yourself home tonight?" Terri asked, noticing the alcohol's effect on Ishmael.

"I don't know. You might have to drive my truck home for

me and tuck me in." Ishmael said feeling horny.

"If I drive you home, I'm a do more than just tuck you in." Terri admitted seductively, staring into Ishmael's eyes.

Ishmael was momentarily speechless, shocked by Terri's aggressiveness.

"Well you know I cook a mean omelet and I would definitely bring you breakfast in bed in the morning." Ishmael said.

"Well I guess I'm a be getting breakfast in bed."

"In that case what time do you get off?" Ishmael asked Terri with images of Terri in the doggy style position racing through his mind.

"I'm off in a half hour." Terri responded, looking behind her at the clock on the wall.

"Aight, that's a bet. But right now I'm a go outside and sit in my truck so I can finish smoking this weed I got."

Ishmael pulled out the half-smoked Dutch Master.

"Oh, you don't have to go outside for that. You can smoke upstairs." Terri said, referring to the second level of the bar where everybody sat around smoking weed.

"That what's up, because I wasn't ready to step outside in that hawk yet." Ishmael said, as he stood up from off of the bar stool.

"Well if its that cold outside you're gonna have to keep me warm tonight," Terri said, wrapping her arms around herself.

"Trust me shit gonna be hot and sweaty tonight." Ishmael said as reached over the bar to rub Terri's chin.

"Well don't be upstairs too long."

"I won't"

When Ishmael arrived at the top of the steps he had to adjust his eyes to the darkness. He found a seat against the wall. The entire upstairs was filled with smoke, as everybody sat around puffing their weed. Ishmael lit up his weed and sat back in his chair, feeling good. For the past few hours he didn't think about Zikeema as much. Terri flooded his thoughts instead.

176

"Damn, I don't believe I'm going home with Terri's fine ass tonight and she thick just like I like 'em too." Ishmael thought, smiling.

As Ishmael continued thinking about going home with Terri, his phone rang, interrupting his thoughts. He saw Zikeema's name and number appear on the phone's screen.

"You fucked up girl. Now you got Terri ready to take your spot." Ishmael thought.

He turned off his phone and placed it back into his pocket. Ishmael inhaled his weed deeply attempting to cloud any thoughts of Zikeema.

"Yo Kyree, what's goin on family?" Doo-Dirty asked as he walked up to Kyree to shake his hand.

"All man, you know if I had your arm I would cut mines off," Kyree said, smiling at his friend.

"Well before you cut your arm off, pass me that weed." Doo-Dirty said as he sat next to Kyree.

"Be careful. This ain't that trash you used to smoking." Kyree said teasingly.

"What? You know I only smoke that top shelf weed." Doo-Dirty said, placing the blunt in his mouth.

"Yeah boy, don't choke on it." Kyree said, watching Doo-Dirty hold the smoke inside his body for as long as he could.

"Dis...dis shit aight." Doo-Dirty said as he allowed the weed smoke to escape through his nose and mouth.

"So what's up wit you tonight?" Kyree asked while Doo-Dirty handed him back his blunt.

"Man, I got this fine ass chick waitin for me to come and scoop her. She half Chinese and half Black, and she got a sister that's finer than her. You tryin to ride over there with me?" Doo-Dirty asked, knowing his partner in crime would definitely be down to go on this mission with him.

"Naw dog, I'm good. I'm a just chill."

"Niggah, did you hear what I said?" Doo-Dirty said, looking

at Kyree like he was crazy. "They Chinese and Black, badder than a muthafucka and I know you can get her sister to drop her draw's tonight."

"I said I'm good." Kyree sat back and continued to smoke his weed.

"I swear man, you been actin real weird lately. What's goin on wit you?" Doo-Dirty asked.

"Man you trippin", Kyree responded.

"Ahhhhh, shit," Ishmael said, as he threw down the blunt he was smoking.

He let the blunt burn down to a roach, which burned his finger tips. He wasn't paying attention to the weed in his hand because all of his attention was focused on the two guys sitting next to him. "Damn...dude called his man, Kyree. Could this be the same muthafucka that's fuckin wit my baby Zikeema?" Ishmael thought with his lip twisted. "Naw, that would too much of a coincidence," Ishmael thought. The feelings he had for Zikeema that he desperately tried to bury suddenly started surfacing again. Ishmael continued to sit there wondering if this was the same Kyree that was causing his heart so much pain.

"Aight niggah, I'm a leave it alone for now, but whatever is goin on wit you, I'm a find out sooner than later," Doo-Dirty said to Kyree.

Kyree just sat back smiling at Doo-Dirty.

"Aight, since you frontin on me I'm a fuck around and pull both of them once I get over there...watch," Doo-Dirty said as he stood up to leave.

"Enjoy yourself pimp and give me a call tomorrow. I got some business to discuss with you." Kyree said, standing up to shake Doo-Dirty's hand.

"Yeah, I'll do that. Stay on your toes out here fam. I'm out."

"You know I will. You just stay on your toes wit dem two sisters."

As soon as Kyree sat back down his cell phone started

ringing.

"Hello."

A smile soon formed on Kyree's face.

"Do I know who this is? Stop playing wit me. You know I know who this is. Halle Berry, right?"

"Pysch, girl you know I'm just playin. You know I know my baby Zikeema's voice when I hear it. What's up with you though?"

"Oh you tryin to see me? You know I'm tryin to see you too. So why don't you meet me at my house in about a half hour."

"Oh, and Zikeema…if you get there before me, you'll find some bags that I bought you. It's just some stuff from Victoria's Secret. Do me a favor and put that lavender set on that's in the bag. I think that set is gonna be my favorite on you.

"OK then. I'll be there in a half, see ya."

Kyree smiled as he hung up the phone. Meanwhile, Ishmael's heart was beating fast in his chest. He couldn't believe what he just heard. Now Ishmael knew it was official. This was the same Kyree, the same Kyree that took his happiness from him, the same Kyree that he hated. "I don't believe this shit. This bitch just was trying to get with me. Now that I didn't answer my phone, she tryin to hook up with this niggah now?" Ishmael thought as he stood up. "Fuck that. I'm a put an end to this shit now." Ishmael followed Kyree down the steps. When Ishmael reached the first floor, Terri called him. But Ishmael walked past not hearing or thinking about Terri. He remained focused on Kyree.

"Yo man can I holla at you for a minute," Ishmael said once he and Kyree were both outside.

Before turning around, Kyree instantly placed his right hand in his jacket pocket, putting it on his gun.

"You talking to me gang?" Kyree said, facing Ishmael.

"Yeah, I'm talking to you." Ishmael said, placing his right hand in his Pelle jacket.

"What's up?" Kyree asked as he looked hard at Ishmael.

"You Kyree, right?"

Before Kyree answered he placed his finger on the trigger of his .44 Bulldog revolver.

"Who wanna know?"

"Zikeema's man wanna know muthafucka."

"Hold up gang. Watch how you talk to me and the last time I checked, Zikeema was my woman." Kyree said.

Kyree figured out that he must have been talking to the same guy that Zikeema often mentioned.

"You think Zikeema is your woman, but I'm here to tell you to stay the fuck away from her." Ishmael said with his palms sweating from holding his gun so tightly.

"Ha..ha, you got me fucked up. So I'm a tell you like this. I'll let you walk away right now unharmed." Kyree said with a menacing look on his face. "But you got to stay away from Zikeema. I'm not in to sharing what's mine."

"You bitch ass niggah, you fuckin with the right one," Ishmael said ready to handle his business.

"Bitch ass niggah, huh? Kyree said, taking a quick glance around.

"Yeah muthafucka." Ishmael yelled.

Ishmael and Kyree pulled their guns simultaneously.

Boom…Boom…Boom…Boom!

"Yeah muthafucka Zikeema belongs to me."

CHAPTER 25

Diamond confined herself to her house for weeks. She let her answering machine take all of her calls. Diamond felt like a hermit, but she knew she couldn't move on with life unless she killed the monster who raped her. That's the only way her mind would be at ease. Diamond finally found the strength to get out of the house. She gathered enough courage to go back to the club. Diamond packed up her Armani Exchange overnight bag filling it wit different go-go costumes. Although she wasn't going to the go-go club to make money, Diamond felt that she should look as normal as possible, so that if the rapist saw her he would not suspect Diamond's motives. She thought that walking around the club in street clothes would bring too much attention to herself.

After her costumes were packed she grabbed her two twin Glocks, checking to make sure that the clips were filled. She finished preparing her guns, packed them, and grabbed her car keys from the table near her front door. She thought about calling Alize', but quickly changed her mind. The last time Diamond talked to Alize' was the night she was raped. Diamond thought Alize' was still mad at her because Alize' never called after that night. "Oh well, I don't have time to deal with her attitude," Diamond thought as she grabbed the bag with the twin Glocks nesting inside.

Diamond had been sitting in her car outside of the club for

the past hour. She was beginning to realize that she wasn't as tough as she originally thought. She was shaking in her boots as she sat in her car. "Girl, stop being a pussy and soldier up," Diamond said to herself. Diamond had a strong urge to smoke some weed to calm her nerves. She then decided not to smoke so that she can be fully aware in the club.

Diamond began thinking about her father, Big Toe. She missed him so much. She missed his presence and his wisdom. She thought about a saying he would use from time to time. "You can back a scared man into a corner, but it's a good chance he might come out of that corner a killer." "Dad you was right about that saying," Diamond thought as she stepped out of her car ready to face her demon.

Fantasy 2000 at 40th and Filbert Streets was packed. Diamond knew there was a good chance the rapist would be there. Before Diamond could get to the dressing room, Strawberry came running toward her.

"What's up girl, how you been?" Strawberry asked.

"I'm good," Diamond said still walking toward the dressing room.

"Girl, I was wondering where you been at. I don't know when the last time I seen you." Strawberry said, unable to tell that Diamond didn't want to be bothered.

"Well, I've been around," Diamond said nonchalantly.

"Sorry to hear about your girl Alize'."

"Alize'! What you mean 'sorry to hear about her'?" Diamond said finally giving Strawberry her full attention.

"Oh, you ain't hear?" Strawberry asked. Strawberry savored the moment. She knew she would be the first to break the news to Diamond.

"I ain't here what?" Diamond asked wanting Strawberry to get to the point.

"Temptation, let me tell you. Remember a few weeks ago at club Playground when they had the New York dancer's come down to battle us?" Strawberry asked.

Diamond's whole body cringed knowing that was the same night that she got brutally raped.

"Y…y…y…Yeah…I remember that night," Diamond said.

"Well, all I know is after the show was over, everybody came outside. We walked around the corner and Alize' was on the ground naked and covered with blood." Strawberry said, wanting Diamond to believe that she was there and witnessed the whole thing.

Strawberry actually stayed home that night. A dancer at the club named Unpredictable called Strawberry that night and told her everything.

"She was naked and covered in blood?" Diamond asked shocked.

"Girl, it looked like she got beat with bats and shovels. We could barely recognize her. I only knew it was her because I seen the teddy bear tattoo she got on her right thigh." Strawberry, said.

"So is she alright?" Diamond asked worried.

"Girl…the ambulance, fire engines, and the police came on the scene. We thought she was dead, but one of the paramedics checked her pulse and said she was alive. Can you believe the paramedic had to scoop dog shit out her mouth? I'm telling you, there's some sick muthafuckas out here these days. They got me ready to leave this dancing shit alone, I'm telling you."

"Do you know what hospital she's in?" Diamond asked ready to check on her friend.

"I ran into Alize's cousin Tracy yesterday and she told me they had her at Temple, but they transferred her to University of Pennsylvania. She told me Alize' had tubes and all kinds of shit running up her nose." Strawberry said with tears in her eyes. "She's hooked up to these machines. Traci says she's fucked up. She's still unable to speak so no one knows who did this to her."

Diamond couldn't help but to feel bad. She believed that if

she didn't leave Alize' that night that Alize' would not have gotten beaten up and she would not have gotten raped.

"I'll be back. I have to use the bathroom," Diamond said leaving Strawberry so that she could pull her thoughts together.

"Maybe I should go home," Diamond thought. The news she received about Alize' took all of the fight out of her. She just wanted to get in bed, crawl under the covers, and stay there forever. "Only if I listened to my sisters, I wouldn't be going through this right now," Diamond thought as she stood in front of the mirror wiping tears from her cheeks.

After ten minutes inside the bathroom, Diamond decided that she would go home. She felt defeated, lost, and unable to think clearly. She washed her hands, splashed her face with water, and left the bathroom.

"Hi Temptation,I know you're not leaving are you?"

"Hi…umm…Corey, right?

"Yeah, I'm surprised you remembered my name."

"I never forget a name or a face." Diamond said as she switched her bag from her right shoulder to her left shoulder.

"That's impressive. So why are you leaving so soon?" Corey asked lustfully staring at Diamond.

"I'm just not feeling well. That's all." Diamond said, wanting to cut the small talk.

"Excuse me. I'm sorry, " a dancer said as she accidentally bumped Diamond while walking past. Diamond's cell phone fell out of her bag hitting the floor. Diamond started to bend down to pick up the phone, but Corey stopped her.

"Please…let me." Corey said, bending down to grab Diamond's phone.

Diamond froze in fear. She couldn't believe what she just saw. Corey's right forearm had a tattoo of a heart with a knife in it. The exact right forearm and tattoo of the man who raped her. There was no mistaking it. Diamond knew she couldn't forget that tattoo.

"Here you go...Temptation, here's your phone."

"Oh...Oh...I'm sorry," Diamond said, grabbing her phone. She continued to stare at Corey's tattoo.

"Ha...ha...ha...you look like you seen a ghost or something."

"I'm fine," Diamond said, trying her best to keep her composure.

"You sure you're OK? Even your hand is shaking." Corey said with a concerned tone.

"Yes. I just think I might be coming down with something. That's all. I think I better go home." Diamond said.

"OK then. You drive safely." Diamond quickly walked off in a hurry.

"Damn. I might got to pay that another visit." Corey thought as he stared at Diamond's curvaceous body walking out of the front door of the club.

"I can't believe I ran into that savage...that...that animal and that he had the nerve to be cool and calm like nothing ever happened, like he didn't brutally rape me," Diamond thought.

Diamond was mad at herself for feeling weak and helpless around Corey. She knew she was going to need some help. Diamond feared that Corey could over power her and rape her again. Diamond took in a much needed breath of air when she finally made it outside of the club.

"Damn shame what happened to your girl Alize'," a voice said from behind Diamond.

"Precious, it was you!"

Diamond turned around and saw Precious and another girl standing behind her holding bats.

"You muthafuckin right it was me. I'm just mad I didn't kill the bitch." Precious said with a menacing look on her face.

"You went to far Precious," Diamond said with fire in her eyes.

"I don't believe this bitch is talking like we don't have bats in our hands."

"You did say she was a little throwed off right?" Precious' cousin Shamia said as she swung her bat around in the air.

"You been ducking and hiding from me for a while now, but you know what Miss Temptation? You can't hide no longer, so prepare for this ass whipping bitch." Precious said to Diamond as she started towards her. Before Precious and Shamia knew what was going on, they had two Glocks pointing at their faces.

"Temptation hold on, please…let's talk," Precious said, dropping the bat and putting her hands up in the surrender position.

"I don't believe you did that to my friend. Then you planned on doing the same thing to me?"

"No…no…Temptation it wasn't like that." Precious said.

"Bitch shut up." Diamond commanded Precious, and you, don't fuckin move," Diamond said to Shamia who was getting ready to run.

"Now look I should kill both of you hood rat bitches. Ya'll got my girl all laid up in a muthafuckin hospital. Ya'll didn't have to take it that far. But you know what? I'm a give ya'll two options." Diamond said with her guns still aimed at their faces. "Ya'll can get a bullet in the head or a bullet in the ass. Now where do ya'll want that bullet?"

"Temptation please wait." Precious begged.

"You don't want me making the choice," Diamond said, pointing her gun at Precious' forehead.

"OK…OK, I'll take a bullet in the ass," Precious said as her bottom lip quivered.

"How bout you sweetie?" Diamond asked, aiming her gun at Shamia's forehead.

"I'll take mines in the ass too," Shamia said defeated.

"OK Precious, since your ass is the fattest, you go first. Now bend over so I can put this hot shit up in you." Precious reluctantly bent over at the waist, as tears rolled down her cheeks.

"Now be still, I don't want a stray bullet going in your spine." Diamond said as she took aim at Precious' right butt cheek.

Pop...pop...pop...pop...pop!

All five bullets meant their mark. Precious fell to the ground screaming in agony.

"Your turn boo-boo," Diamond said to Shamia.

"Wait a minute. I thought you said you was going to shoot us once in the ass?" Shamia asked nervously.

"I never said how many ass shots ya'll was getting. Now if you want to get shot once, I can shoot you one time in the head." Diamond said with a grin on her face.

"No...no...no...I'll still take my ass shots," Shamia started to bend over.

Pop...pop...pop...pop...pop!

Diamond shot her right and left butt cheek before Shamia could bend over completely. Shamia fell on top of Precious.

"Next time ya'll won't have this option." Diamond explained, bowing down over Precious and Shamia.

After putting her guns back in her bag, Diamond calmly walked to her car. Diamond pulled out her cell phone to call her cousin.

"Hello, may I speak to Baby...Baby, what up girl? It's me, Diamond."

"Girl, I know my cousin's voice. What's goin on stranger?" Baby asked while blowing weed smoke out of her mouth.

"I got a problem and his name is Corey."

"Say no more. Me and Rozelle will meet you at your house in an hour," Baby said.

Diamond smiled after hanging up. "Corey better enjoy life now, because Baby and Rozelle were on their way." Diamond thought. She knew her cousin Baby and her friend Rozelle were cold-blooded killers. Diamond heard police sirens nearing. "Someone must've called them about shots being fired." Diamond thought, as she started her Benz. She pulled off, driving past the police. "The cops are always late. I guess they are a joke." Diamond said to herself as she cracked a little smile.

CHAPTER 26

"Do you think she'll like this one?" Skeam asked his flunky Redz.

He already knew Redz would say yeah.

"Yeah, She'll love that one." Redz said, looking at the 10 carat ring that Skeam held.

"Yeah Redz, I think you're right. She should love this one." Skeam said, looking at how the lights bounced of the flawless Diamond.

"Skeam, I don't want you taking this the wrong way, but you don't think you might be movin a little fast," Redz said with a concerned look on his face.

"You know Redz, I thought about this for a long time and I've come to the conclusion that Stori and I are meant to be together. I mean when people would talk to me about love at first sight, soul mates, and shit like that, I would look at them like they was crazy. But ever since Stori came into my life, she completely changed my way of thinking. She showed me that there is a such thing as love at first sight and soul mates. The only way I really can explain it to you is, she completes me. That's why I'm a make it official and ask Stori to marry me."

Redz seemed happy on the outside, but on the inside he was mad as hell. All of his action was slowly going down the drain thanks to Stori.

Skeam knew people would be talking shit behind his back,

but he didn't care. He was happy. In a few of his past relationships Skeam felt that he was in love. Now he realized that those past relationships were never true love. Stori showed him the meaning of true love. Skeam thought about Stori from sun up to sun down. There wasn't a moment in the day that went past where thoughts of Stori weren't flooding Skeam's mind. Skeam's raps seemed to be getting softer, more about love. He went from having a hard and gritty rhyming style like DMX to having a style like L.L. Cool J, who rhymes strictly for the ladies. But the only lady Skeam was rhyming for was Stori. Now Skeam found himself in a jewelry store doing something he thought he would never do. Skeam bought Stori a ten carat engagement ring and a tennis bracelet that held ten carats worth of diamonds. As Skeam left the jewelry store and continued walking down Jeweler's Row, he felt like the happiest man in the world.

*****

"Damn, I can't even find Emani. I already know that damn Tori and Zikeema is ducking my calls. How can I be mad at them when I've ducking their calls too?" Stori thought as she hung up her phone. Stori had a plan. She would get all of her sisters together and break the news all at once. Then she would pull Zikeema and Tori to the side to tell them that robbing Skeam was off. Stori thought that they would understand and be happy for her. "But if they don't like how things are going, too damn bad, because I love my Skeam." Stori continued in thought.

Ding-Dong...Ding-Dong

"This better be Zikeema or Tori," Stori said, walking towards her front door.

"Oh, Hi baby. I thought you was my sister," Stori said, surprised to see Skeam.

"Sorry for not calling first, but I needed to see you," Skeam said, munching on a bag of Skittles candy.

190

"There's no need to be sorry. I'm glad you're here."

"Can I come in?" "Boy stop playin and get in her." Stori pulled Skeam into her house and gave him a long wet kiss.

"I miss you baby," Skeam admitted, embracing Stori's body.

"I miss you too and your timing couldn't have been better," Stori said after breaking away from the embrace.

"I totally agree because we need to talk," Skeam said, popping more Skittles into his mouth.

"Have a seat. I'll be right back."

Stori went into her bedroom for a few minutes to collect her thoughts. "This is it girl. Just tell him how you feel and let him know he's going to be a daddy," Stori thought. She sat on the edge of her bed trying to understand exactly how she would tell Skeam the news.

"Baby, you forget I was out here or something?" Skeam hollered from the living room.

"No, here I come," Stori announced, leaving her bedroom.

"Boy, you out here acting like you missing me or something," Stori said as she reached the living room.

"You know I am. Come over here and talk to your man." Skeam pulled Stori down on his lap.

"I need to talk to you about something, but I don't know how you're going to react to it." Stori said, rubbing her fingers across Skeam's chest.

"I need to talk to you about something also."

"What you gotta talk to me about?" Stori asked.

"No, you first."

"OK, " Stori said. She took a deep breath. After a minute went by, Stori began to speak.

"I uhhmmm…had an appointment today."

"What kind of an appointment?" Skeam asked, holding Stori's hand.

"I had a…uhhmmm doctor's appointment."

"Is everything ok?"

"Yes. Everything is wonderful for me, anyway," Stori said, looking down and playing with her finger nail

"Well what's the problem then?"

"Look I can't tell you no better way but to come straight out and tell you. My doctor said I'm pregnant, so you're going to be a daddy."

A sudden sense of relief came over Stori.

"You're? I'm a be…I'm a be a father?" Skeam stuttered.

"Yes, you are," Stori said, looking into Skeam's eyes.

Skeam picked Stori up from his lap and spun her around in the air.

"Boy put me down."

"I'm sorry. Did I hurt the baby?" Skeam asked letting Stori go and rubbing her stomach.

"No you didn't hurt the baby," Stori said laughing.

"I'm a be a daddy!" Skeam said smiling from ear to ear.

"Well, I'm glad to see you're happy."

"Why wouldn't I be? I'm having a baby with the woman I'm in love with," Skeam said, doing the Whopp dance.

"Boy you silly," Stori said, happy that Skeam was excited.

"So what do you have to tell me?" Stori asked.

"I wanted to tell you how much I love you. Even though we haven't been together that long, I know you are the one for me. So what I'm trying to say is hold up, where's my bag of Skittles?"

Skeam picked up his bag of Skittles and started eating them again. Stori sat there with a look of wonder on her face. "Skeam was just pouring his heart out to me now he's worrying about some damn candy," Stori thought, becoming pissed at Skeam.

Skeam poured some more candy in his mouth before continuing…

"What I want to know is…"

"Skeam what's wrong with you? Baby…baby, are you alright?"

Stori suddenly realized that Skeam was choking on the Skittles. Stori got behind him and started performing the Heimlich maneuver. After pumping Skeam's stomach for the third time, something shiny flew out of Skeam's mouth and landed on the couch.

"Are you OK, baby?" Stori asked with a worried look on her face.

"You saved my life, baby," Skeam said smiling.

"What was that that flew out of your mouth?" Stori asked as she walked over to the couch.

Stori picked up the shiny object. She was surprised to see that it was a ring.

"What's this?" Stori asked, looking confused.

"It's yours if you'll marry me...Stori, will you marry me?" Skeam asked bending on one knee. Stori stood there shocked and momentarily speechless.

"Well?"

"Yes, baby yes, I'll marry you." Stori started crying.

Skeam stood up and gave his wife-to-be a hug.

"Boy I should kill you. You had me thinking you was choking." Stori said while looking at the ring on her finger. "I don' believe you had the ring in that Skittles bag. This is so beautiful. Even though you got candy juices all over it. Now walk me to the kitchen so we can wash this off."

CHAPTER 27

Zikeema and Tori sat in Zikeema's basement going over the plan to rob Skeam.

"So what you sayin', we goin' to the front door and ringing the bell?" Tori asked, making sure she heard Zikeema correctly.

"Yes, we are. I got these from Jamal. We're going to put these on and they're goin to invite us in." Zikeema said, pulling out two authentic gas company uniforms.

"That damn Jamal can get his hands on anything," Tori said, referring to their childhood friend. Tori held up the gas company uniform for a brief inspection.

"Plus, we got a gas company work van, so we should have no problem pulling this off." Zikeema explained as she took her street clothes off.

"Now once we get inside, all we want is the money and jewelry that's in the safe."

"How do we even know he has a safe with money in it?" Tori asked while changing into her gas company uniform.

"I know we are going in on this a little blind, and you can thank your twin sister for that, but come on. Skeam's a young black man that's a rapper and a millionaire. I know he keeps a bunch of money in that house." Zikeema expressed confidently.

"Yeah, you're probably right. But I'm still messed up in the head about Stori leaving us high and dry."

"Well except it and get your head straight. She shitted on us now, but we'll shit on her later when we got a table full of money in front of her."

In her mind, Zikeema already had a trip to Las Vegas planned after she robbed Skeam.

Ring…Ring…Ring…

Tori sees Stori's name and number appear on her cell phone. "Speaking of the devil."

"That's Stori? Don't even answer. Matter of fact, let me turn my cell phone off now before she tries to call me next."

"Yeah, we'll get with her later on when we're counting them dead presidents in front of her face."

"Damn Tori. Your butt looks like one of those Luke dancers' butt in them pants."

"I can't help it if these pants fit my round ass nice. Besides, Jerome love's it." Tori said, running her hand across her voluptuous butt.

"All I know is if these uniforms don't get us in the door, that fat ass of yours will," Zikeema said playfully smacking Tori on her butt.

Zikeema and Tori loaded their .40 caliber handguns, placed their guns in a tool box, and headed toward Skeam's house in the gas company van. Skeam's house was located in Gladwyne, a small town outside of Philly, home to many of Philly's athletes and celebrities.

"These houses is beautiful and they're so big," Tori said, looking out of the van's window.

"Yup, and that's the big ass house we ready to run up in," Zikeema said, pointing to Skeam's immaculate home.

"Yeah girl, with a house like this, you gotta have some change up in there." Tori couldn't take her eyes off of Skeam's six bedroom four bathroom house, with a pool, Jacuzzi, basketball court, and well-kept lawn the size of a football field.

"Look, when we get to the front door, I'll do all the talking. You just stand on the side and look like a gas company worker."

Zikeema explained.

"How the hell does a gas company worker look?" Tori asked while pinning her hair into a bun.

"Girl I don't know, but figure it out, and here, put this on."

Zikeema handed Tori a baseball style gas worker's hat and a pair of cheap sunglasses. Zikeema and Tori lowered their hats down onto their heads as far as they could. With their cheap sunglasses on, Zikeema knew their disguises would be good enough. She believed that once the .40 caliber handguns were shown all the attention would be on the guns and not their faces.

"Hold up Zikeema," Tori said with a worried look on her face.

"Tori you better not be having second thoughts," Zikeema demanded ready to get her master plan rolling..

"No…no, you know I'm wit it, Stori just popped into my head."

"Why is you worrying about her for? I thought we came to the agreement that we was doing this without her." Zikeema said wanting desperately to prove that she could mastermind a robbery as good as Stori.

"No girl, I'm not talking about that, but think for a minute. Stori's been going out with Skeam for a minute, right?"

"Yeah, and so…"

"And so, look at me and look at Stori. Have you forgot? We are identical twins. I can't go in there with just this hat and sunglasses on. He's going to think I'm Stori from the door."

Zikeema stood there dazed thinking about what Tori had just said. She couldn't believe she overlooked the fact that Tori and Stori looked exactly alike.

"Maybe I'm not a master planner," Zikeema said to herself.

Zikeema's second thoughts on robbing Skeam exited her mind as quickly as they entered. She snapped out of her daze and began thinking about the robbery.

"Look, take this and put it on," Zikeema said, pulling out a black ski mask from her bag.

"Now there's going to be a small change in plans. I'm a go up to the door myself, as soon as you see me enter the house, come right in behind me, aight?"

Zikeema handed Tori her gun from the toolbox.

"I'll be right behind you sis." Tori said, gripping her gun.

After grabbing the toolbox and a clip board, Zikeema headed towards Skeam's front door.

Skeam stood in the shower singing along to R. Kelley's song, *12 Play*. He was preparing to meet Stori's sisters so that he and Stori could announce their engagement. Skeam still couldn't believe what Stori told him earlier. "I'm goin to be a dad! I'm goin to be a dad!" Skeam yelled out in the shower. He knew that his life was headed toward a drastic change. He was ready to embrace that change.

Skeam got out of the shower and started getting dressed.

"Excuse me, Mr. Skeam. There's a gas company worker at the door." Carmen, Skeam's Hispanic housekeeper, announced through Skeam's closed bedroom door.

"Carmen, just let him in and see what the problem is," Skeam said.

"Yes sir, Mr. Skeam."

"Yes, may I help you." asked Carmen.

"Uhhh…yes, there's a gas leak in the neighborhood and we were going door to door checking everybody's house making sure everything was safe. Uhhmmm…Is the owner of the house in." Zikeema asked, looking down at the clip board.

"Yes, he's upstairs. Come in and I'll go get him."

Carmen stepped to the side to let Zikeema through the front door. Zikeema walked through the door observing the inside of the house. Zikeema knew right away that Skeam had good taste.

Carmen tried to shut the front door, but Tori quickly stopped her.

"If you make any noise, I'll blow your pretty little head off," Tori said to Carmen. Carmen stood there frozen in fear.

"Do as we say and you won't get hurt. Understand?" Zikeema asked while pulling her gun out of the toolbox.

Carmen couldn't speak, but Zikeema read Carmen's eyes and knew that she wouldn't be a problem.

"Now, where is Skeam?" Zikeema asked. Carmen just focused on the black leather gloves that were wrapped around the handle and trigger of the .40 caliber hand gun.

"Do I have to repeat myself?" Zikeema asked.

"No...no, no, he's upstairs getting dressed."

"Who else is in the house?" Zikeema asked as Tori peaked out of one of the windows.

"No one. Just me and Mr. Skeam."

"Well take us to him," Zikeema commanded, jamming her gun in Carmen's back.

With Carmen leading the way, they eventually reached the top of the steps where they could hear R. Kelley playing loudly. Zikeema walked up to the closed bedroom door and put her ear upon it. She could hear nothing but music.

"You ready?" Zikeema asked Tori.

Tori nodded her head up and down while gripping her gun tighter. Zikeema pushed Carmen into Skeam's room first. Behind Carmen was Zikeema and behind Zikeema, Tori. Skeam's back was turned so he didn't realize that Carmen, Zikeema, and Tori entered the room. Tori walked over to push the off button on the stereo. Skeam turned around realizing someone was in his room.

"You see these guns, so you know what it is." Zikeema said as she and Tori pointed their guns at Skeam. "Don't make me turn this robbery into some blood shed. Now where the safe at?"

Skeam couldn't believe what he was seeing. He didn't know if the stick-up was a joke or a real robbery.

"I don't know what you're talking bout," said Skeam.

"Do you think you'll figure it out after I put a bullet in this bitch's head?" Tori said, placing the gun on the side of Carmen's head.

"Wait…wait, I got a floor safe under my bed," Skeam admitted quickly.

"Well let's get to it." Zikeema said, waving her gun at Skeam.

Skeam was filled with anger, paranoia, and confusion. He still couldn't believe what was going on, but did what he was told. Skeam used his right had to push the bed over, while keeping his eyes glued to Zikeema and Tori. He slipped his left hand under the pillow that was on the bed. Skeam's eyes expanded as he felt the barrel of his 9 millimeter Taurus hand gun. He had forgotten that he placed the gun under his pillow the night before. Skeam started thinking about Stori and the baby. He knew he had to do something. Tori walked over to Skeam and saw the floor safe.

"We gotta a safe!" Tori announced excitedly, looking toward Zikeema.

Skeam's confidence grew as he maintained a tight hold of his gun. With speed like a cheetah, Skeam slipped the gun from under the pillow and aimed it at Tori. Tori smiled under her ski mask as she continued to look in Zikeema's direction. Tori soon noticed Zikeema's facial expression turn from happiness to fear. Tori looked away from Zikeema and turned her attention toward Skeam. Tori swallowed hard as she was now looking down the barrel of a 9 millimeter hand gun.

CHAPTER 28

"I swear on everything I love, this niggah Corey gonna wish he was never born when I'm done with him." Baby said to Diamond.

Diamond had explained to Baby and Rozelle about the rape. Baby was still hyped after hearing about Diamond's horrific experience. She paced back and forth while psychotic thoughts of violence ran threw her mind. In Baby's eyes, what Corey did to Diamond was only punishable by death, a nice, slow, and agonizing death.

Rozelle pulled out a rolled up Dutch Master cigar filled with purple haze weed and lit it. After taking a few puffs, she passed the cigar to Baby so that Baby could calm down. Usually Baby was always calm and in control. But, when it came to her loved ones, Baby went crazy. She would lose all control to the point of even killing someone.

"What is wrong with these sick muthafuckas out here? You know what though?" Baby said, inhaling the purple haze. "Im a find this pussy and show him how sick I can get, watch."

Rozelle sat quietly in her chair smiling to herself. She wondered what Baby had in mind for Corey. Whatever it was, Rozelle couldn't wait to get the party started. Baby and Rozelle were two beautiful women whom you did not want to cross. Their innocent appearances made them look harmless. That was one of the main reasons why they were two of the top contract killers in the country. In the past, they've been hired by local drug dealers, the Russian mob, the Chinese mob, the Italian mob, and host of others. Killing missions were never personal for Baby and Rozelle as long as the money was right. Diamond was family for Baby. As far as Baby was concerned, nobody fucked with family, nobody.

"So we the only ones you told about this?" Rozelle asked Diamond, finally breaking her silence.

"Yeah, I haven't told my sisters or nobody," Diamond said with her head held in shame.

"Good, keep it that way, cause we gonna handle this sick dick head tonight. So the less people that knows, the better." Baby said, cracking her knuckles.

"Diamond pick your head up. We about to go hunt this piece of trash down and do him dirty." Rozelle said.

They all grabbed their bags to head toward the strip clubs. They hit every strip club in the city that night. Hours were spent in The Kee, The Grind Stone, Rock's Lounge, Bottom's Up, The Playground, Night On Broadway, Fantasy 2000, Uncle Sam's, The Blue Velvet, and Picadilli's, before ending at Dutch Gardens on 5th and Luzerne Streets.

"We've been all over the city looking for this piece of shit," Baby said, sitting in a chair upstairs in Dutch Gardens.

"At least we made some money tonight," Rozelle said as she counted the money she made from lap dances.

"I know. I see why you be dancing Diamond. I could get used to this." Baby said as she and Rozelle shared a laugh.

Baby noticed Diamond's laughter was cut short by Diamond's stare across the room.

"Diamond what's wrong?" Baby asked.

Diamond, unable to talk, just pointed across the room.

"What Diamond, what's up?" Baby continued.

"That's Corey right there in the red shirt," Diamond said.

"Oh yeah?" Rozelle said with a slight grin on her face.

"Look, I don't think he saw you so sneak outta here and meet us at the spot. We'll have his ass over there in about a hour." Baby said.

Diamond left the club undetected. Baby and Rozelle made their way over to Corey. When they were in Corey's view, Baby and Rozelle started dancing with each other, feeling and rubbing on each other's body. Corey was instantly hooked. He stared at Baby and Rozelle. They stared back. Mesmerized by their beauty, Corey made his way over to Baby and Rozelle.

"Hi handsome," Rozelle said.

"Hi yourself," Corey replied, rubbing his goatee. "Ya'll looking real good tonight. What's ya'll name?"

"I'm Horny," said Rozelle.

"and I'm Untamable," said Baby.

"Are you really horny or is that just your name?" Corey asked, with his mouth watering.

"Both," Rozelle answered, seductively looking back at Corey.

"Horny and Untamable, huh...I like that," Cory said, looking back and forth between Baby and Rozelle. So what do I have to do to get your fine ass to spend up all my money?" Corey asked Baby.

"If I'm a spend up your money, Horny has to be involved also," Baby responded, walking up to Corey and grabbing his crotch.

Corey got an instant erection. He felt that this had to be his lucky night.

"So, is we getting outta here?"

"I thought you'd never ask," Rozelle said to Corey.

"Look, don't you get lost. We gonna change real quick and we'll be right back, OK." Baby said as she rubbed the side of Corey's face.

"I ain't goin nowhere. I'll be sittin right here." Corey said, pointing to one of the metal folding chairs.

Ten minutes later.

Corey, Baby, and Rozelle were standing outside in front of the club.

"So what hotel ya'll wanna go to?" Corey asked, hoping they did not choose an expensive hotel.

"Honey, you don't have to spend your money. We got a crib like 15 to 20 minutes away from here." Rozelle said. "Besides, that's where all our toys are at."

Corey stared at Rozelle's erect nipples through her thin shirt. "OK, that'll work. Ya'll drivin?" Corey asked.

"Naw. Our girlfriend dropped us off." Baby said.

"Aight, let's be out then," Corey said, leading the way to his car.

Twenty-seven minutes later.

Corey, Baby, and Rozelle pulled up to a house in Southwest Philly.

"I hope you ain't no two minute brotha," Rozelle said, teasing Corey as they approached the house.

"Naw, I took my ginseng today, so I'm ready to put in over time," Corey said.

"Yeah, we'll see," Baby said as she unlocked the door to the house.

"Have a seat handsome, while we go slip into something more comfortable," Rozelle said, while she and Baby headed upstairs.

Five minutes later.

Baby and Rozelle came down the steps wearing sexy lingerie. Corey's eyes doubled in size while watching the two beautiful women walk over to him. Baby and Rozelle sat on opposite sides of Corey squeezing him in tightly.

"I want you to know that we are both freaks, so I hope you're down with what we're down with," Rozelle said, rubbing between Corey's legs."

"I'm…I'm wit it," Corey managed to get out.

"Well, let's go upstairs, so we can get this party started," Rozelle said.

"Hold up. Let me get the whip cream out the refrigerator first," Baby said.

Baby went to the kitchen and came back with a can of whip cream. They all went upstairs. When Corey stepped into the bedroom he noticed two pair of handcuffs on the bed near the headboard with another two pair at the foot of the bed.

"Damn, these two are some freaks," Corey thought to himself.

"Strip!" Baby commanded.

Corey started taking off his clothes.

When he got completely naked, Baby ordered him to lay on the bed. Corey anticipated the time of his life. Rozelle straddled him and grabbed his right hand so that she could handcuff him to the bed.

"Hold up, Horny. I'm not into that tying up shit." Corey said to Rozelle.

"I thought you said you was freaky like us? Besides, when I'm sucking your dick and Untamable is licking your balls, I don't want you trying to stop us." Rozelle said, licking her full juicy pink lips.

With that statement by Rozelle, Corey stopped thinking with his big head and started thinking with his little head.

"Fuck it, handle your business," Corey said, spreading out his arms.

After Rozelle cuffed both of Corey's hands and feet, he laid spread out on the bed.

"You ever had a threesome before? Baby asked Corey as she crawled up on the bed next to him.

"Yeah, I experienced this once or twice before," Corey said, smiling.

"Have you ever been with three women at once?"

"Naw, I can't say I have."

"Well, you know what? You're in for a treat tonight. Yo Diamond!"

Diamond walked in the room with a pair of vise-grips in her hand and a look on her face showing that she was ready to kill somebody. Corey's body stiffened. He didn't believe that Diamond just walked in the room.

"You remember Diamond don't you or should I say, Temptation?" Baby asked Corey, with an evil grin on her face.

"Uhh, yeah, yeah. How you doin Temptation?" Corey asked Diamond. Diamond stood there staring at Corey.

"You know I don't think she got no rap for you, being as though you raped her and all," Rozelle said while pulling out a bag filled with an assortment of tools.

"Raped her? I didn't rape her." Corey said.

"Pussy tell me the truth!" Rozelle said, placing a pair of pliers around Corey's big toe. "I swear every time you lie, I'm breaking one of your toes. Now did you rape her?"

"I didn't."

Snap.

"Ahhhggghhh," Corey cried out, having his big toe broken.

"Scream all the fuck you want. I own the houses on each side of this and they are abandoned. Plus, I got this room sound proofed last week, so nobody can hear your bitch ass. Now, I'm a ask you again. Did you rape her?"

"Wait!"

Snap.

Rozelle broke another toe.

"Yo this niggah is gonna be fun. Let me turn my hype music on." Baby said, putting her DMX cd in the stereo.

After she pushed play, Baby sang along to the song and began to do the running man dance. *"Ya'll goin make me lose my mind,*

*up in here, up in here/ya'll goin make me act a fool up in here,
up in here..."*

Rozelle and Diamond broke out laughing.

"Go Baby. It's your Birthday," Rozelle and Diamond chanted
over and over again.

Corey looked among the three women with fear in his eyes.
It felt like a nightmare to Corey as he laid there in unbearable
pain watching the girls run, jump, laugh, and joke around him.

Corey thought, "If I could only get my hands and feet out of
the handcuffs, I could overpower them and cause them the same
pain that they're causing me."

Corey soon realized that with all the wishful thinking he
was still helpless. He just prayed the he would make it out alive,
because if he did there would be hell to pay for the girls.

"I wish you could get up and dance with me, but I know it
would be kind of hard trying to do the two-step with them broken
toes. Matter fact, go 'head and break another one Rozelle." Baby
instructed, as she switched from the running man dance to the
Steve Martin dance.

Snap.

Snap.

After the fourth broken toe, Corey would have told on his
own momma.

"I'm sorry, Temptation. I swear I'm sorry for raping you.
Please forgive me." Corey begged, hoping that his last six toes
stayed in tact.

"What da fuck you say, forgive you? Pussy, do you realize
what you did to me?" Diamond asked Corey. "I don't think you
do, but you know what, I'm a make sure you never do it again."

Diamond grabbed a taser gun hitting Corey in the testicles.
She tasered Corey's testicles repeatedly. Then she decided to
concentrate on the left testicle. She eventually put the taser gun
down and grabbed the pair of vise-grips. She placed the vise-
grips around Corey's left testicle and squeezed down. Corey

made a sound of an animal that is only found in remote areas of the jungle. Diamond repeated the same thing to Corey's right testicle. It flattened out between the vise-grips. Corey passed out. Corey woke up to Diamond slashing him all over his body with a box cutter. Blood was everywhere.

"I got an idea. Here Diamond, use this." Baby said, handing Diamond a box of salt.

Diamond poured the salt in every cut she made on Corey's body. Corey screamed out in agony. His torture lasting for hours.

"Who else you rape, pussy?" Diamond asked Corey, as she continued pouring salt into his cuts.

Corey laid there unable to speak or move. He didn't know how much more he could take. He felt pain from his head down to his toes. With so much pain and injury, no one would be able to recognize Corey.

"What else can we do to him? We all ready broke all his toes and fingers. We broke a few bones in his face. We cut him from head to toe. We crushed his little nuts. We pulled all his teeth out..."

"Now that was fun..." Rozelle admitted, interrupting Baby.

"Yeah that was fun, wasn't it? I'm just trying to figure out what else we can do to this bitch ass niggah?" Baby said, running out of ideas.

"I know, when the pussy raped me he wanted me to suck his dick. He ain't try that shit though, cause he knew I would of bit that shit off." Diamond explained, with an evil look on her face. "So since he likes his dick sucked, I'm a let him suck it."

"Girl, what you talkin bout?" Rozelle asked.

"Let me see that bag of tools you got." Diamond asked Rozelle.

Diamond looked through the bag until she found what she needed. She pulled out a large pair of shears.

"Is you about to do what I think you're about to do?" Baby asked with her devilish grin.

"You know it." Diamond said as she walked over to Corey's half-dead body. Diamond started hacking away a Corey's penis.

The shears she used were very dull, so she had to put some muscle into her work. Finally, the penis fell in a pool of blood that had settled between Corey's legs.

"Damn Baby, your cousin is more vicious than you are," Rozelle said, enjoying the show.

Picking the battered penis up from the bed, Diamond stuffed it into Corey's mouth.

"You feel better now?" Rozelle asked Diamond.

"You know what? I do feel better." Diamond answered, looking down at Corey's mutilated body.

"Well, I don't. Watch out..."

Boom...Boom!

"Now I feel better. I don't want his mom being able to have an open casket." Baby said. With two shots to Corey's face from her 12 gauge shotgun, Baby shot off half of Corey's head.

"So what are we gonna do with him?" Diamond asked.

"Don't worry about that. I'll call up my clean up crew. They'll handle everything. Go 'head and take them cover-alls off." Baby said, giving Diamond a hug. "Go home, take a hot bath, and just relax. I'll call you tomorrow."

"Aight, I'll do that." Diamond said, smiling ear to ear with satisfaction.

CHAPTER 29

Stori kept staring at the 10 carat pear shaped Diamond ring that had found a home on her left ring finger. With Skeam accepting the news of her pregnancy and proposing to her, Stori wondered when she would wake up from her dream. Six months ago if someone told Stori that she would be pregnant and engaged to the man she loved with all of her heart, she would have laughed in his or her face. Never in a million years would Stori had thought she would be getting married and having a baby.

Kids and the married life was never Stori's style. She always said that her kids were her nieces and nephews. She took them out, spoiled them rotten, then dropped them off at their mother's. Stori always thought that there wasn't a man in the world that was on her level, a man that could check her and put her in her place when she needed it, a man to take charge of a situation. Stori had found the perfect man. Her Skeam passed all of her test with flying colors. She liked how he was sensitive and strong at the same time. She loved how he carried himself like a king and treated her like a queen.

"Diamond, what you doin?" Stori asked Diamond over the phone.

"Nothin, I just made me a steak-um sandwich. I'm a eat that and watch a movie coming on the Lifetime channel. Why, what's up wit you?" Diamond asked, grabbing the ketchup out of her refrigerator.

"I need to gather everybody up. You talk to Zikeema or Tori today?"

"Naw, I haven't talked to neither one of them in a couple days." Diamond explained, grabbing the sour cream and onion potato chips from her cabinet.

"I've been calling both of them all day and I keep getting both of their voice mails."

"Girl, I don't know what to tell you." Diamond said with potato chips crunching in her mouth.

"How about Emani? I've been getting her voicemail too."

"I talked to her a few days ago. Why what's goin on?"

"It's nothing to worry about. I just need to get everybody together, so I can make an announcement." Stori said, excited that she finally was going to tell her sisters about her and Skeam.

"Stori what you got to announce?" a nosey Diamond asked.

"Look, just meet me at my house in two hours. I'll find everybody else by then and then I'll make my announcement. You got it?"

"Yeah, I got it. I just hope it's some good news, because I don't need no bad news."

"Just be there in two hour and you'll find out then."

"Fine," Diamond said, sucking her teeth.

"Bye, you big baby," Stori said, teasingly.

"Bye."

Stori got into her car and headed to Emani's house. After finding out that Emani wasn't home, she then went to Zikeema and Tori's house. They weren't home either. She decided to head over Skeam's house to see if her baby was ready to meet her family. The ride to Skeam's house was twenty-five minutes. She sang along to 112's song *Cupid*, feeling happy and in love. She felt like this was the happiest day in her life and that nothing could change that. Stori even thought about giving up on the stick-up game. "After all, I'm a be a wife and a mother," Stori thought to herself, rubbing her still flat stomach. "Damn, I hope this baby doesn't make me too fat. Do you hear me? Don't make mommy fat. Thank you Skeam for coming into my life." Stori thought as she continued to rub her stomach.

Stori pulled up to Skeam's house and parked behind a gas company's work van. She still hummed *Cupid* as she exited her car. "Damn, I got the keys to Skeam's heart and this big ass home." Stori thought, as she smiled. Stori held the diamond encrusted heart shaped key chain that Skeam gave her. "I can see me living in Skeam's beautiful home," Stori thought as she floated up to Skeam's beautiful home. Stori felt like she was on cloud nine. Stori opened the door to find the house completely quiet. "Let me sneak up on my fiancé. Damn, I like the way that sounds, fi... an...ce'..." Stori thought as she headed up the steps.

When she made it to the top of the steps, Stori tiptoed up to Skeam's bedroom door. Stori couldn't believe her eyes when she looked into Skeam's bedroom.

"Put the fuckin gun down or I'm a drop this bitch," Skeam said to Zikeema, holding his gun to Tori's head.

"Keem, don't drop shit. If you drop your gun this pussy gonna shoot both of us." Tori said, continuing to stare down the barrel of Skeam's gun.

"Wait...please wait," Stori said, running into Skeam's room.

"Baby, get out of her, run! These muthafuckas is trying to rob me." Skeam said, worrying about Stori's safety.

Stori ignored Skeam's demands and walked over to Zikeema.

"Keem, put the gun down," Stori said, placing her hands on Zikeema's shoulders.

"Naw...fuck that, Stori. You see this niggah got his gun on Tori." Zikeema said, hiding behind Carmen. Zikeema inched toward Skeam with Carmen in front.

"Stori, what the fuck is going on, you know these people?" Skeam asked, with a confused look.

"Yes, baby...these are my sisters, Zikeema and Tori, I've

been telling you about." Stori said calmly.

"I...I don't understand. What is this, some kind of joke or something?" Skeam said looking at Tori, then Zikeema, then back at Stori.

"Listen, everybody put their guns down and let's talk." Stori said, pleading with everybody.

"Tell this muthafucka to drop his gun first," Tori said.

"Yeah Stori, let this niggah know I will shoot him right between his eyes," Zikeema said, holding her gun steady.

"I can't do that Keem."

"What da fuck you mean you can't do that? Do you see what da fuck is goin on in this bitch?"

"Yes Keem, I see what's going on. I can't do that though because he's my fiancé and the father of my unborn child I'm carrying now in my stomach." Stori said.

Zikeema and Stori stood there in complete shock.

*****

"Are you serious, how's Skeam gonna marry chic? He barely knows her." Popcorn said to Redz as they sat in Skeam's Yukon Denali smoking weed.

"Yeah man, this bitch Stori is fuckin up everything. Skeam is wide open about this hoe. We don't go out no more or nothing." Redz said, letting the weed smoke escape from his nostrils.

"The stupid bitch even got us in here drinking forties of Old English 800. Since we don't go out no more, I haven't had any Cristal or nothing." Popcorn said, missing how they would only drink Cristal when they went out with Skeam.

"I still don't know how this money hungry bitch Stori got her hooks in Skeam. I'm a put an end to that shit though." Redz said, taking a sip of his forty ounce beer.

"Skeam is too far up this bitch ass for you to change that. You not gonna be able to end it." Popcorn said, not believing Redz could get things back to normal.

"Niggah, don't ever doubt my skills. If I say a duck can pull a truck, muthafucka, hitch em up." Redz said.

"Well, I hope you can do something, because I'm having a drought like a muthafucka. I need to get my dick wet. You know I'm addicted to them groupies." Popcorn said, thinking about all the beautiful women that would settle for him after Skeam turned them down.

Popcorn, Redz, and the rest of Skeam's flunkies were all affected by Stori coming into Skeam's life. None of the flunkies liked Stori, especially Redz. The parties, free food, free drinks, beautiful women, and the many other perks they enjoyed were no more. All the flunkies blamed Stori.

Redz sat in the truck scheming on how he would end the headache named Stori.

"Redz, what you gonna do smoke all the weed?" Popcorn said, breaking Redz from his daze.

"Muthafucka you over there doin all that cryin...what the babies gonna do? Besides, this my weed niggah." Redz said to Popcorn.

"You know I got the next bag," Popcorn said, always trying to get high for free. "Here man, take this weed and get out." Redz said, handing Popcorn the half-smoked blunt.

"Redz, you know I'm just playin wit you. Why you kickin me out?" Popcorn said. I gotta shoot over to Skeam's crib, so I can handle some business for him. When I'm done I'll be back to get that bag of weed on you." Redz said, knowing Popcorn wouldn't have two nickels to rub together.

"Aight Redz, I'm a be right here at my mom's crib waiting on you," Popcorn said, stepping out of the truck.

"Aight, I'm a get at you," Redz said as he drove off in Skeam's Denali.

"Yeah, this bitch gotta go," Redz thought.

Redz walked into Skeam's house as he always did.

"Where the fuck is Carmen? She gonna give me some of that Puerto Rican pussy, with her fine ass." Redz said to himself as he headed upstairs to Skeam's room.

Once he reached the top of the stairs, Redz heard various voices coming from Skeam's room. The voices did not sound friendly to Redz. Redz creeped up to Skeam's doorway and peaked in. He quickly pulled his head back with out no one noticing him.

"What da fuck is goin on there? I know they not in there tryin to rob my homey or something." Redz thought, pulling out his Calico .9 millimeter from off his hip.

"I know Skeam is gonna bless me with something nice after I handle this shit for him and finally I can get rid of this bitch Stori once and for all." Redz thought as he stood in the hallway holding his gun with both hands.

After Redz took three deep breaths, he charged into the room.

"Skeam watch out!" Redz said, firing his gun.

One of Redz' bullets struck Carmen in the back of her head missing Zikeema by inches. After that everything seemed to move in slow motion for Skeam, Tori and Zikeema as they watched Stori's body drop to the floor.

"Nooooooo!" Skeam, Tori, and Zikeema yelled in unison. They all emptied their guns on Redz hitting him twenty-seven times between his body and head. Skeam, Tori, and Zikeema dropped their guns and ran over to Stori's fallen body.

"Baby, hold on." Skeam said, cradling Stori in his arms as he looked at all of the maroon colored blood covering Stori's shirt.

"Somebody call the ambulance!" Tori yelled with tears rushing down her face.

"We don't have time for that. I'll take my wife-to-be to the hospital myself," Skeam said. Skeam picked up and carried Stori to his car.

Tori and Zikeema followed close behind.

A HUSTLER'S WORST NIGHTMARE

Eight months later:

Bobbi cried relentlessly. She didn't think she had so many tears in her body. For the past several months she was a total wreck. Bobbi knew she made the biggest mistake of her life by going to see Chicken Neck Merlino. Bobbi could never forgive herself for that. She made it through the attempted murder with only a few cuts caused by the bullets going through the car's window. Emani wasn't so lucky. She caught four bullets in her back trying to protect Bobbi.

It was killing Bobbi inside knowing that the shooting was all her fault. "If I wasn't so jealous and so much in a rush to get me and Emani's relationship out in the open, all this never would have went down," Bobbi thought as she rocked back and forth in her chair. Rocking back and forth was a nervous habit that she picked up after the shooting.

"Bobbi will you stop all that crying," Emani said, waking up in her hospital bed.

All Bobbi could do was give Emani a half smile as tears continued to stream down her cheeks.

Since the shooting occurred, Bobbi stayed by Emani's side. She didn't want to leave Emani for a second, not even to go to the bathroom. Since Emani was back in her life, Bobbi knew that she would have to take her secret to the grave.

"Please baby, can you stop crying for me? You acting like this your fault or something. Baby, this is not your fault. This was a random thing and there was nothing you could do about it." Emani said, reaching up to wipe a tear off of Bobbi's face.

Bobbi cried harder. Emani's words were killing Bobbi inside. Bobbi was willing to do anything to keep Emani in her life.

"Excuse me ladies, do ya'll have a minute," Detective Jaworski asked as he stuck his head inside Emani's room.

"Yes, Detective Jaworksi, come on in," Emani said, looking toward the detective.

"How are you feeling?" Detective Jaworksi asked Emani as he approached the side of her bed.

"Besides these bed sores I've been getting, I'm doing alright."

Detective Jaworksi had a special place in his heart for Emani's circumstance. The same thing happened to his sister a few years ago. With all the killings and shootings that were happening in Philadelphia, the police detectives would have thrown Emani's file toward the bottom of the heap along with countless other files. But Detective Jaworski dedicated himself to bringing Emani's shooter to justice. It was a personal matter for Detective Jaworksi.

"Well, I don't want to hold you up. I just wanted to come by and let you know there still isn't any leads, but I'm not giving up." Detective Jaworski said with pen and pad in hand. "I just wanted to make sure that there's anything you remember. I mean even the smallest details might help me find this loser."

"I'm sorry detective, but I still don't have any memory of that day." Emani said.

"That's ok Miss Cooper, just get better. How about you Miss Parker? Do you remember anything?" Detective Jaworski asked Bobbi.

Bobbi put her head down before answering the detective.

"No detective. Like I said before, everything happened so fast, I didn't get a chance to look at the shooter." Bobbi said, just wanting the nightmare to go away.

"Ok ladies. I won't hold ya'll up no longer. If ya'll do remember anything please give me a call." Detective Jaworski said.

"I will." Emani replied.

The detective left and Emani and Bobbi were alone. Bobbi would never tell the detective that she could identify the shooter. The thought that the mob would come back and finish the job had Bobbi scared to death. For Bobbi, telling the detective who the shooter was meant certain retaliation by the mob that would silence she and Emani forever.

Emani began laughing for no apparent reason.

"What's so funny?" Bobbi asked as she reached for tissue to blow her nose.

"I was just thinking about the day I was shot. My mom always told my sisters and I to always keep on clean underwear in case we got in an accident or something and had to go to the emergency room."

"So, you always keep on clean underwear," Bobbi said with a hint of sarcasm.

"I know, but if you remember that day, I didn't have on any underwear at all." Emani said, chuckling.

Bobbi managed to laugh a little between her tears and sniffling. She hadn't seen Emani cry once. She couldn't believe how Emani was holding up under her horrific circumstances. Although Emani was one of the strongest people she knew, Bobbi was a total mess.

*****

"Hey girl, what's goin on in here?" Zikeema asked as she, Diamond, and Tori walked in carrying a bunch of flowers and balloons.

"Nothin. I'm just trying to get my baby to stop crying over here." Emani said, reaching up to wipe tears of Bobbi's face.

"Hi." Bobbi said to the sisters as her head remained down and tears continued to fall.

"Is my sister-in-law feeling better?" Tori asked, placing her arm around Bobbi's shoulder.

"I'm doing a little better." Bobbi said, wiping her nose.

All of the sisters met Bobbi after the shooting. They all immediately warmed up to Bobbi and embraced Emani's lesbian relationship with her. Bobbi also felt a strong sense of comfort being around Emani's sisters. Bobbi liked all of them.

"Look at ya'll. Ya'll look good together." Diamond said.

Emani smiled with relief knowing that her sisters accepted her relationship and whole-heartedly liked Bobbi.

"I'm telling ya'll now. When ya'll get married I'm a be the maid of honor." Tori said, putting her bid in first."

"Yeah right!" Zikeema and Diamond said in unison.

As Tori, Zikeema, and Diamond argued over who would be the maid of honor, Emani and Bobbi watched and laughed.

"I love you baby," Bobbi said, looking into Emani's eyes.

"I love you too," Emani said, grabbing Bobbi's hand and kissing it.

*****

Stori and Skeam stood in the elevator holding each other. Stori explained everything to Skeam. She told him how she and her sisters were planning to rob him, but she fell in love instead. Skeam was hurt at first, but his love for Stori was too strong for him to let go of her, so he forgave her.

"Baby, do you still love me?" Stori asked.

"I love you for the rest of my life," Skeam said, bending down kissing Stori on her forehead.

"But, I can't have kids anymore," Stori said, putting her head down and wiping a tear from off her cheek.

"I'm a love you forever, baby. Won't nothing change that." Skeam said with his hand placed under Stori's chin. He lifted her head up so that he could kiss her.

Before Redz lost his life, he managed to shoot Stori once in the stomach killing her and Skeam's unborn child. Stori made a full recovery from the shooting. The only thing Stori didn't recover from was the emotional injury of losing her child and being told that she will never have kids again.

Everyone was laughing when Stori and Skeam walked into Emani's room.

"Ya'll in here all loud and ghetto. I heard ya'll all the way down the hall." Stori said.

"There go my sister and brother-in-law," Emani said with a smile.

Everybody exchanged hugs.

"Now this is like big family reunion," Diamond said.

"All we're missing is Uncle Flea," Stori mentioned as the room quieted.

"I'm a miss him," Tori said with her head bent and playing with her fingernail.

"I still can't believe he's gone." Zikeema added.

"I do know this, with everything that went down with our family, I know Uncle Flea would have wanted ya'll to stop all the stick-ups and stuff." Emani said, looking around at all of her sisters. "So can ya'll please promise me ya'll stop robbing people."

They all promised to stop.

"And Tori don't worry about Jerome. I know he'll come back into your life. You two had a wonderful marriage and some beautiful kids. He's just feeling betrayed right now, but he'll be back." Emani continued.

Emani knew Tori was hurting with Jerome out of the house. Jerome found out about Tori's secret life.

"I know. He's just so damn stubborn. He's not goin nowhere. I got him too whipped." Tori said, wishing that her marriage was not over.

"Well, whatever you do, get back with your husband. He's a good man." Emani said. "And don't worry about me. I promise I will walk again."

Emani was paralyzed from the waist down.

"We know you'll walk again." Everyone said at different intervals.

"Hold up ya'll. Somebody turn that up." Stori said.

Bobbi grabbed the remote turning the volume up on the TV.

"Hi This is Lori Johnson. I'm here; down at Penn's Landing, where the police have found the mutilated body of an unidentified man. Police sources say that they believe the unidentified male victim is the infamous Fairmount Park rapist. The police say his body was wrapped up in plastic, that his genitals were cut off and stuffed inside his mouth. At this time, the police are continuing their investigation. When we get more information on this case, we'll be the first to get it to you. This is Lori Johnson reporting for Fox news."

Bobbi turned the volume down on the T.V.

"See that's what a person like that gets," Zikeema said, shaking her head.

"I definitely don't have no pity for him," Stori remarked, snuggling closer to Skeam.

Diamond sat off to the side of the group with a slight smile on her face. She knew exactly who the unidentified body was. Much like Stori, Diamond had no pity for the unidentified man.

"Is this where the party at?" Kyree asked, as he stuck his head inside of Emani's room.

"Hey baby. What took you so long? You know I was missing you." Zikeema said, getting up to hug Kyree.

"I'm sorry babe, but I talked to Emani earlier and she told me she was dying for a cheesesteak from Jim's. So you know I had to hook my girl up." Kyree said, holding a brown paper bag.

"Thank you Kyree. You're the best." Emani said, extending her arms toward her cheesesteak.

Kyree looked around and loved the scene he saw. The love and care that everybody showed one another was something he never experienced growing up with drug addicted parents. He vowed to himself to love and keep Zikeema forever. Zikeema could never find out that it was him who killed Ishmael. Kyree was there to console Zikeema as she grieved for Ishmael. After Ishmael' death, Kyree and Zikeema's relationship grew stronger. Kyree knew if the truth ever came out he would lose Zikeema forever and that was something he never wanted to happen.

"Hmm, the smell of that cheesesteak is getting me hungry. I'm about to walk to the vending machines. Anybody want anything?" Diamond asked as she stood up to stretch.

Diamond took everybody's order. Zikeema and Tori decided to go with Diamond to help carry the food back to the room. They walked to the elevator joking and laughing.

Diamond's pace slowed as she witnessed a familiar face standing at the opposite end of the hallway. The familiar face was talking to a doctor. Diamond continued walking toward the familiar face as Tori and Zikeema remained near the elevator. As soon as Diamond reached the doctor the familiar face turned to face Diamond and the doctor walked away.

"Girl, I thought that was you. How you doin Alize'?" Diamond said surprised at Alize's appearance.

Diamond barely recognized Alize'. She had on a long church dress, her hair was pinned up, and she wore no makeup on her face. Diamond was used to seeing Alize' in scantily clad provocative outfits only. Diamond was futher thrown off by the bible Alize' held in her hand.

"By the grace of God, I'm doing well and how are you?"

"I'm doin great. Look at you though Alize'. You changed so much." Diamond said, looking Alize' up and down.

"Diamond no disrespect, but please call me Laraine. Alize' died a year ago on that sidewalk."

"I'm sorry. I meant no disrespect, either." Diamond said with her head down.

"That's ok Diamond. The last time you seen me that's what you was calling me, so you didn't know." Laraine said, placing her hand on Diamond's shoulder.

"I was so sorry when I heard about what happened to you," Diamond admitted, noticing the scars on Laraine's face.

"Thank you, but that was just a wake-up call for me that I truly needed. When I was in that coma, God came to me, opened up his arms, and embraced me. Right then and there I knew everything was going to be alright. When I woke up from my coma, I realized it wasn't about serving me. It was about serving God. I was living in sin chasing after that money, not realizing I was running away from my savior. Now I know ain't nobody perfect and I don't want to stand here and preach to you, but Diamond you really need to get out of that game. That money those men throw at you is not worth your self-respect. Just do me a favor and open up your eyes. I guarantee you'll see that dancing isn't worth the aggravation. I'm only telling you this because I love you like a sister and God loves you even more."

Diamond saw the sincere look in Laraine's eyes.

"I hear you Laraine and I'm a definitely take all of that into consideration," Diamond said.

"That's good Diamond. You'll see life will be so much better. Well, I hate to cut our meeting short, but I have to get to my therapy." Laraine said as she checked the time on her watch.

"OK, Laraine. It was good seeing you. Make sure you keep in touch."

"I will."

Laraine and Diamond hugged. Then Laraine limped away. Diamond stood there for a moment watching Laraine. She still couldn't believe how much Alize' had changed.

"Diamond, is you comin girl?" Tori yelled from the other end of the hall.

"Oh..oh, here I come." Diamond said, walking back toward her sisters.

"Who was that?" Zikeema asked Diamond as they all entered the elevator.

"Oh, that was just an old friend I haven't seen in a while." Diamond explained.

So, what we gonna do ya'll?" Tori said while pushing the "L" button on the elevator.

"Look ya'll, I feel everything that Emani was saying in the

room, but I got this niggah lined up already. His money is longer than the crack of a fat bitches ass and robbin him is gonna be sweeter than cotton candy." Zikeema said. "So, if ya'll wit it let me know. I'll make that happen."

"Am I wit it? Do a fat kid like all kinds of treats? Hell yeah I'm wit it." Diamond said, thinking her dancing days may be truly behind her.

"I'm still not where I need to be to retire, so count me in too. I'll deal with my husband later." Tori mentioned.

"I guess some things never change." Zikeema said to Diamond and Tori.

They walked out of the elevator with dreams of getting paid. They definitely were every hustla's worst nightmare.

THE END

MEET THE AUTHOR

Derrick King currently resides in Philadelphia. He's the CEO of KingPen Publications.

He is currently working on his second novel, *City of Brotherly Thugs.*

Email him your feedback on A Hustler's Worst Nightmare. He would love to hear what you have to say.

Email address: kingpenpub@yahoo.com

From The Bestselling Author of
"Paper Doll" Comes A Story
of Heartbreak, Scandal
& Getting Even!

A Novel By: Nicolette

ORDER FORM

Name: _____

_____

Address: _____

_____

City/State: _____

Zip: _____

QUANTITY	TITLE	PRICE
	A Hustler's Worst Nightmare	$15.00
	Shipping	FREE

TOTAL $_____

Send check or money order to:
KINGPEN PUBLICATIONS
P.O. Box 28037
Philadelphia, PA • 19131